Oc

Daniel Euphrat

Part 1

Out in the slums on the south side of town, some old man cut himself open from pelvis to sternum and tried to divine the future from the pattern of his own entrails.

This left Tom and me with the unfortunate job of cleaning up the mess. That was our job, cleaning up dead bodies.

"'The Gods have ordained,'" Tom read from a blood-stained scrap of paper, "'as reflected in the fractal microcosm of the universe that are' he crossed out 'is' here and wrote 'are,' 'that are my bowels, that the future shall be as follows: lots of bad things are going to happen.'"

"That's it?" I said.

"That's all the guy wrote yeah. Maybe he died before he was finished," said Tom, adjusting his facemask.

"Well shit," I said, "I could have told you that without cutting myself open."

"Yeah," said Tom.

"Stupid old fucker," I said. "Come on, let's gather him up."

We scooped up the main body and the large chunks and piled them into the body bag as best we could.

There are probably regulations on how to do this sort of thing, but at the company we worked for no one bothered to tell us and we didn't bother asking.

Next, we started in with the abrasive chemicals and sponges and started scrubbing.

"He drew a bunch of stuff all over the walls, it looks like," I said loudly so that my voice would carry from the bedroom to the living room. "Do we have to clean that off too?"

"Not unless it's drawn in blood or other… bodily substances," Tom called back.

"Looks like chalk," I said.

I came back into the living room where the body and most of the blood seemed to be.

"He drew a lot of pictures of jellyfish on the walls," I said.

"Weird," said Tom.

About halfway through, Tom stood up with an exasperated sigh, shaking bloody soap off his gloved hands and wiping them on his disposable plastic apron. "I feel like a smoke," he said. "You feel like a smoke?"

"I don't smoke, you know that," I said.

"I don't mean cigarettes."

"Oh. Then yeah."

We probably could have smoked out in the living room, but it seemed like we shouldn't. We decided to find a more secluded spot. The house was a mess. There were flakes of off-white paint all over everything. A door hung attached by one hinge. The hardwood floors were warped, and there were holes here and there.

"I don't really want to go up these stairs," I said.

"Dude, let's do the basement! I bet it's creepy as fuck," said Tom.

"You have to use stairs to get to the basement," I said.

"Yeah but you're going down, not up. So you

wouldn't fall as far."

I laughed.

We went down into the basement. The stairs made horrible creaking sounds, but they didn't collapse. There were indeterminate piles of things everywhere that I didn't want to look at too closely. There was a rack of shelves with jars on it. There were dark objects floating in the jars. Again, I didn't look too closely. There was also a room with two toilets, at right angles to each other. One was covered with some kind of tarp, the other was half destroyed. The light bulbs flickered and dangled from wires.

"Don't be a pussy," said Tom, carefully stripping off one glove in a way that turned it inside out, then used that to take off the other glove, and reached under his layers of protective smocks and aprons to pull out a little sneak-a-toke and lighter.

"I wasn't complaining," I said, reaching to take the thing from him before I realized I still had my own bloody gloves on. I took them off.

"Yeah but I can sense your pussy-ness," said Tom. He thought for a moment. "I'm very good at detecting pussy, you know."

"I hate to break it to you, man, but I have a dick. So if you've relied on this method in the past…"

"Shut up and smoke that shit."

I pulled my mask off my nose and worked on getting the lighter to light.

As I did this, Tom paced around, kicking at various piles of things.

"Careful, man, one of those things might…" I trailed off into a coughing fit.

Tom laughed. "See I told you you're- holy shit, dude! Check this out!"

One of the piles Tom had kicked had been covering a fairly large hole in the concrete that opened into blackness. Not completely black though; if you focused, you could see a flickering orange light and at the opposite side, a little ways down, a ladder.

I told Tom that the whole thing was a bad idea as I was stretching out over the hole, with him holding on to my belt, reaching for the ladder. I knew it was a bad idea right from the start.

"Don't you want to go adventurizing?" He said.

"Not really," I grunted. The broken concrete was digging into my stomach.

I managed to grab the ladder and pull it over. It was metal, just a normal ladder like you'd buy at a hardware store, but old and rusted. It made horrible creaking and grinding noises as we climbed down.

"We should have gone one at a time," I said. "I could swear we're tilting slowly to one side…"

"We're almost there, I think," said Tom. "Don't worry. But I mean… don't slow down either."

And then we reached the bottom. It was stone, not concrete, but solid stone like you'd see in a cave. It was kind of chilly, and the air was very dry and dusty. We followed this tunnel for a while, lit by more flickering bulbs strung along the ceiling. The tunnel sloped down and down and zigzagged and meandered. I have no idea how far it went, but it felt like we were following it forever. We passed what looked like really old rusted mining equipment, carts and pickaxes, and some kind of big drill bits.

***

Gradually, we noticed another pulsing glow over the flickering light bulbs, a deep red glow. And then the tunnel opened into a massive cavern and we were caught with a blast of tremendous heat. Stalagmites maybe ten or twenty feet tall sprouted from the ground and you could see similar stalactites hanging from the ceiling far above. Some connected in giant pillars. Massive, I don't even know how big. Like redwoods.

There was the wreckage of some kind of giant drilling machine, bigger than a semi. Catwalks and riggings spanned the air above us, and hung down in tangles and crisscrossed the pulsing red pools of lava. Or magma, whichever it was. The air reeked of horrid, burning smells which I guessed were sulfur and brimstone or something similar.

We followed a path worn in the stone out into the cavern. We weren't really talking anymore at this point. The path meandered between the lava pools.

And finally, impossibly, the cavern opened into an even larger cavern and we were at the shore of a lake that went off as far as the eye could see into the dark. Except the water here wasn't clear like water, it was pure white.

And floating up and down in the water in front of us was a wide, flat-bottomed boat attached to a thick chain that was attached to a beaten down pulley machine. The chain stretched off over the lake into the darkness.

We looked at each other for a moment and then there was this loud click and a metallic thumping sound started that got faster and faster until it turned into a whiney grinding sound, and I realized Tom had pulled the lever on the pulley machine, and then we realized that the chain had started moving, and we splashed into the milky liquid to jump onto the boat before it pulled too far away.

We rode the boat for what seemed like a very long time. We steadily picked up speed until we were moving at a pretty good clip, at least based on the breeze on our faces. It was too dark to see how fast we were moving. The cool air felt good after the stifling heat of the lava pools. The white liquid had just kind of run off our clothes, it didn't really absorb. The air was moist and had some strange smell that almost seemed familiar but I couldn't place. Sort of like chemicals, but sort of sweet.

I couldn't help but think about some Greek mythology I'd read once, about people being taken by boat to the land of the dead.

After some time, I was dozing off a little when the boat scraped up on the opposite shore with a terrible scraping noise worse than fingernails on a chalkboard.

We climbed off. The cave went on for a while more, and then it ended. It was just a solid wall of rock, with one small rectangular opening carved in it the size of a door, and in it was a metal grate like you see on elevators in old apartment buildings. And sure enough, it was an elevator.

We got inside and closed the door. There was only one button, with an arrow pointing down. Not much of a surprise I guess... Tom pushed the button and it went down.

I'm not sure how long we were in free fall. I was glad then that I'd smoked that weed. I probably would've gotten sick otherwise. And then gravity slowly started to return and got stronger and stronger until my legs burned with the strain of trying to stay on my feet and then with a final jolt it was over.

Through the metal grating and a haze of dust, we could see a pale white glow. Not an electric glow either; almost like daylight, but not quite.

"Well fuck," said Tom. It was the first time either of us had spoken in a long time.

***

I opened the grate and we stepped out through the haze onto hardwood floor. Flecks of off-white paint floated in the air with the dust disturbed by the elevator's arrival. It was a house. The elevator had dropped us off in what looked like a bedroom. Walking out into the living room, I half expected to see half-cleaned blood spatters and our cleaning supplies and what was left of the old man piled in a bag. But it was empty. Just hardwood floors, flaking off-white walls, windows covered by some kind of cloth or maybe white plastic bags, with a run-down staircase to our left.

"Well this is a hell of a thing," said Tom.

"I'm confused," was all I could say.

***

"Fucking Lizard People, man," Tom said. "Don't you read the internet?"

We stood stupidly on the sidewalk for a while, just looking around. It was just like a normal city, just like the one we'd left god only knows how many miles above. Except cleaner. Not really cleaner, though, there was plenty of debris lying around, plastic tarps, random metal things, but it was somehow barren. Everything was white or grey or black. The trash wasn't normal city trash, it was like what you'd see at a construction site. Plastic tarps and metal rebar.

The buildings were fairly standard multistory buildings except the building we'd come out of, which looked like a rundown apartment building except it stretched way, way up into the sky, disappearing in a point up above. And the sky: it was blue, but not the right color of blue. And all of it was the same color. There were no clouds, and no sun. Light radiated equally from everywhere. It was as if the sky were just a giant glowing dome. Which would make sense, since we were underground and all.

Tom had decided it was Lizard People.

"I'm telling you," he said. "Hollow Earth Theory? There's this race of lizard aliens that control everything on Earth, politics and business and everything. And guess where they live? In fucking cities miles under the fucking ground. That's where we are man, Lizard People city!"

"You read this on the internet?" I said.

"Yeah, just for fun. I never really thought it was true. But come on! What the hell is this then?"

"I guess we should look around and see if there are any Lizard People down here then," I said.

"Fuck that," said Tom. "We're leaving now. We're going back up there, and we're going to tell like the military or something and get them to cram a nuke down this fucker."

"But we-"

"You're right! They run the military too! Fuck!"

"The Lizard People do?"

"Of course. Well shit I don't know what we'll do, but I know we should leave right fucking now."

"We're already down here, we should take a look around," I said.

"Do you know what those reptilian bastards will do if they catch us? Do you?"

"Something bad?" I said.

Tom made an exasperated noise.

I knelt down and picked up a scrap of pale grey plastic. It had no logos or writing on it. No marks of any kind.

"Look, man," said Tom. "You can stay down here and get turned into a Lizard People egg incubator, but I am not down for that shit. I'm getting my ass out of here. I'm going to go back up and tell, like, the police or I don't know who. Goddamn it, the police have to be Lizard People central too. Well, I don't know who I'm going to tell but I am definitely doing the first part. The part where I leave."

"Ok," I said.

He sighed. "You aren't coming?"

"I'm going to look around some more," I said. "I'll come back up in a bit."

"You do know you're doing that thing that people always do in horror movies right before they die, right?"

said Tom.

"Maybe life isn't a horror movie," I said.

Tom shook his head. "If it's any kind of movie it's a horror movie. Or have you forgotten what we do eight hours a day?"

I dropped the plastic and stepped out into the street. There was no wind, but the air didn't seem stale. It smelled like fresh air and sawed wood, like a construction site.

Tom turned back to the house. "Well," he said. "Good luck, I guess. Give me a call if you make it back up in one piece." He didn't sound hopeful.

"I won't be down here for too much longer," I said.

"Yeah, I bet," said Tom. He glanced around nervously one last time and went back into the house.

He slammed the door behind him. The sound triggered something in me. I suddenly felt very small and alone.

I stared at the house for a moment, my eyes following it up and up into the blank blue sky. Then I turned away and began to walk.

***

The streets all looked basically the same: blank gray buildings and empty sidewalks. No street signs either. I figured it would be easy to get lost, so I just kept walking in a straight line. Blue wires stretched from building to building like power lines.

I was looking up at the wires, the tops of the buildings and the fake sky when I felt something crunch under my shoe. I stopped and looked down. Broken glass. It looked like a shattered bottle. There was a rectangular label with glass stuck to it. I picked it up carefully. There was no writing on it, just a blue circle on a white background.

And then I realized something was different. There was a strange quiet buzzing sound. It sounded mechanical, but it wasn't a simple machine hum. It moved and shifted as it echoed down the side street to my right.

I stood up. I looked back the way I'd come, then back in the direction of the sound. The side street looked as empty as any other. I broke my straight line rule and took a right.

"Left at the broken glass," I told myself. Easy enough.

As I walked, the buzzing grew louder. It seethed like a cloud of electric hornets. I remembered what Tom had said about the mistake characters always make in horror movies. That made me nervous, but I kept walking, glancing both ways down each intersection I passed.

As the buzzing grew louder, the sound became more distinct and complex. I had never heard anything like it. It was like a symphony being played by an electric razor. I turned left at the next intersection, following the sound. After another block, it was on my right. I turned again. I was walking faster now. I rounded the next corner and stopped so abruptly I almost fell over.

There was a woman. She was sitting on the sidewalk a few buildings down, one leg folded under her, the other pulled up against her chest. She was resting her cheek on her knee, staring down at the ground, and turning a crank on a small red speaker box that buzzed and buzzed as she cranked it. Shoulder-length white hair shrouded her face.

She looked up at me, startled. My insides froze. For a second I wanted to run, but I found that I couldn't move.

She was beautiful.

She stared at me for a moment, confused. Then she waved. She said something, but I couldn't hear her over the buzzing red box.

"What?" I called back.

She cranked the box backwards and the buzzing ground to a halt. My ears rang in the sudden silence. She said something in a language I didn't recognize.

"I don't understand," I called back.

She laughed. "I said 'hello,'" she said.

"Oh," I said.

"What's your name?" she said.

"Jordan," I said.

Her name was Lilith.

Lilith was small and very pale. Her eyes were silver.

"What is this place?" I asked her.

"What do you mean?"

I wasn't sure how to form the question.

"What are you doing down here?" I asked.

She shrugged. "Making sounds," she said, gesturing at the small red speaker box.

"Why? What does it do?"

"Only... makes sounds?" she said. "You turn the crank and the sound comes out. Want to try? Do you like the sound?"

"I kind of do, yeah," I said. "So that's the only reason you do it? Because you like how it sounds?"

"Yes," she said. "Sometimes people give me money because they like it too."

"So there are more people down here?"

"Not that many on this street," she said. "I think I chose a bad place."

"Are the other people... like you?" I said. "What will they do if they find me here? Is it not safe for me to be here?"

She looked confused. "Safe? I don't understand you. Are they like me? What do you mean?"

"I'm sorry," I said. "I'm... not from around here."

She laughed, flashing her teeth. "Then where are you from?"

I flinched and stepped back.

"What's wrong?" she said.

"Your teeth..." I said.

She reached up and touched her mouth. She touched the sharp points of her teeth with her fingers. "What is it? What's wrong with them?"

"I... uh... nothing," I said.

"Don't make fun of my teeth," she said.

"I'm just... I'm not used to seeing teeth like that. They look... dangerous."

"They're not dangerous," she said. "Don't make fun of me."

"I wasn't trying to make fun of you. I was just surprised. My teeth aren't like that, see? Mine are flat. Yours look like you could really hurt someone if you bit them."

"I wouldn't bite you," she said.

"Yeah, please don't do that. But you see my teeth? See how flat they are? That's all I meant. I wasn't trying to make fun of you. Your teeth probably work way better than my teeth. For, like, biting things. Like food, I mean. Not people. Listen, I'm sorry. I don't understand any of this. I was at work and then we found this weird basement and this elevator. And now there's a whole city underground and you and I don't understand any of it. I don't understand it. And you know, I should probably go back now. Yeah, I think I'm going to go back."

I started to back away.

"Wait," said Lilith.

"I don't understand any of this," I said, "and I want to go home now."

"Don't go home," said Lilith. "I wouldn't bite you. Please stay. I don't understand either. Where was the basement? Please don't go. Do you want a beer?"

"What?" I said.

She reached into a small cloth bag behind the red box and pulled out a bottle. It had a white label with a blue circle and no text. "You can have this one," she said.

"What is it?"

"It's beer. Do you like beer?"

I stared at her for a moment, then I started laughing.

She smiled, then covered her mouth with her hand. "Don't be afraid of me," she said. "I'm giving you a beer. That means I'm a nice person, not scary."

"I don't think you're scary," I said.

"Then stay," she said. "Drink and talk to me."

I laughed. She handed me the bottle.

"Sure," I said. "Why not? What could possibly go wrong?"

***

"I know that house," said Lilith. "The very tall house that goes up and up."

"Yeah, that's the one," I said. "I mean, probably. Unless there's more than one."

We were walking down deserted streets. Lilith had put her drone box into the cloth bag with the few remaining beers.

"I only know one tall house," said Lilith. "I think... I can't remember."

I had mentioned I was hungry, so she was taking me to a food station. I felt like we had been walking for a long time, but I wasn't sure. The light never changed.

"My friend Tom freaked out and left as soon as we got here," I said. "He thinks there's something bad down here."

"Something bad? Like what?"

"I don't know. Like an army of bad people or something. He said Lizard People."

"I don't know what this means," said Lilith.

I laughed. "Me neither. I think he's just being paranoid. I sure as hell haven't seen an army down here."

"Army?" Lilith chewed thoughtfully on her lip. I was amazed she could do that without hurting herself. "I don't know about these things. I don't think there's anything bad here. The computer wouldn't make anything bad."

"What computer?" I said.

Lilith raised an eyebrow at me. "The computer that made everything."

"A computer made this?" I said.

She laughed. "Where you come from, they don't know?"

"First I've heard of it," I said.

"If you don't know about the computer, how do you think everything was made?"

"Like this place down here? No idea. Or like everything everything?"

"I only know one everything," she said.

"The big bang, I guess? But a computer built this place? How? Why?"

"Because the computer loves us and wants us to be happy," said Lilith. "Because it wanted to make us, so we could be happy."

"But who made the computer?"

"I don't know," Lilith chewed on her lower lip. "Maybe a person? But then who made the person? Another computer? Another person? You can keep asking forever. I think about it sometimes, and sometimes it's fun, but sometimes I don't like thinking about it. When I think about asking questions forever sometimes I get scared."

"Yeah," I said. "I know the feeling."

"It's not good to be too much in your head," she

said. "That's why the most important thing is that the computer loves us. Then you can just feel it and not think and you don't have to keep going forever. You can rest in the feeling."

"I guess that makes sense," I said.

"See? You don't have to be scared. There aren't bad people who want to hurt you here. People here are nice."

I didn't say anything.

Lilith stopped walking and touched my arm, turning me to face her. "Do you think I'm a bad person?" she said. Her silver irises caught the light and flashed. Her pupils were vertical slits like a cat's. Or a lizard's.

"I don't think you're a bad person," I said. "I think you're very... nice."

She smiled up at me. "See?" she said.

***

The food station was semicircular counter protruding from the side of a building, shaded with a bright blue awning. Lilith typed something into a keypad. A small door at one end of the counter slid open and a small grey robot wheeled out with a bowl of soup. It was followed by another small robot with a round loaf of golden bread on a plate and another small robot with six beer bottles in a plastic bucket. The robots delivered their goods, rearranged themselves in a tightly choreographed maneuver and wheeled out another small door on the other end of the counter.

Lilith giggled. "The robots here are so cute."

"Yeah, that was pretty adorable," I said.

"Here," Lilith pulled out some spoons from a slit in the counter. "The food is good too. Eat some."

The soup was the perfect temperature. It had chunks in it that were halfway between meat and tofu. It tasted like flowers and cinnamon and lemon.

"Don't we have to pay first?" I said.

"No, you don't pay for food. Do you have to pay for food where you come from?"

"Uh, yeah. You have to pay for everything where I come from. That's why I work eight hours a day at a job that I hate rather than sit on the corner and play a music box all day."

Lilith laughed. "It sounds like you don't have fun there."

"I kind of don't," I said.

"It's more fun here. You only need money for really fun things," she tore off a piece of bread with her hands, then tore that piece in half and handed one half to me.

"Like what fun things?" I said.

She looked at me for a moment, chewing, a small smile on her lips.

"I like fun things," I said.

"Do you like melting?" she said.

"Like melting how?"

"Melting like seeing time," she said. "Like being its breath." She moved her fingers like a wave.

"These fun things sound like my favorite kind of fun things," I said.

She reached into her jacket and brought out a small vial of white liquid.

"What is it?" I said.

She leaned in. "Milk," she said, her mouth a few inches from my ear.

"Do you think I can maybe try some of this Milk?" I said.

"I'm not sure…" she said. "Milk isn't like food. I have to pay money, remember?"

"I have money," I said. "But I don't think it's the right kind of money."

"Maybe I can give you some. As a favor. Because I'm a nice person."

"That would make sense," I said. "You are a nice person."

"And then," she slid her free hand up under my shirt, "maybe you can do something for me. As a favor." Her fingers played across my ribcage.

"I, um, well," I said. "That might just work. Assuming, I mean, that when you say favor…"

She kissed the corner of my mouth.

"I don't mean something bad," she said. "I promise."

***

I was lying on clean white sheets, hands folded behind my head, staring at the black box on the ceiling. The boxes were everywhere, just posted on walls and ceilings. Just a little black box, no blinking lights or anything, and a blue wire running out of one side. They all had the blue wire. This one snaked along the ceiling and down the wall and into a tiny hole.

"What are you thinking?" Lilith asked me as she wriggled back into her pants.

"Don't know," I said. "These fucking boxes are everywhere down here. It creeps me out."

She laughed. Her pointy teeth only made her look cuter. She was uniformly pale from head to toe.

"Don't worry about that," she said.

"What are they though?"

She shrugged. "I don't know."

I laughed.

"Why are you laughing?" she said, coming up to the side of the bed and putting her hand on my arm.

"Nothing, just thinking…"

"Well," she said, climbing up to lie on top of me, "you should stop that."

"Laughing? Or thinking?"

"Yes," she took out a tiny bottle of Milk and unscrewed the top, sucking a tiny bit up with the dropper. "Open your mouth," she said.

"Aaaa," I said and felt the drop land on my tongue. It burned a little, then filled my mouth with a bitter, chemical taste.

"Now close your mouth," she said, "and don't move."

A second drop fell on my closed lips and she leaned in to lick it off.

A warm and excited feeling was spreading in my stomach. Things on the periphery of my vision began to melt, so subtly at first it might be a trick of the eye but then stronger and stronger. Melting, pulling outwards.

"You feel it?" She said. Her face was still a few inches from mine, lit from the left by white light. The contrast between light and shadow was becoming more defined.

I opened my mouth to say something but forgot what I was going to say. Her eyes glinted like mercury. I could see the vertical slits widening. I could see every perfect detail in the iris of her right eye, a crumpling silver landscape under a clear dome. I felt wet all over, my hands and head and body all displaced. A ripple crawled over her hair and over her face. Every moment was flowing into the next like a liquid, tiny shifts in the delicate muscles of her face, the curling wisps of white hair perfectly clear for a fragment of a second before melting into the next in an endless cascade. I saw her and the room all at once, one crystal clear, intensely three- dimensional moment. We were in a tiny dollhouse viewed in extreme close-up, a picture of a model of a house shot with a stereoscopic camera, everything frozen in time except for us.

"You feel it?" She said and then she was kissing me. I felt lips and hands but I couldn't tell where they were or which were mine. We were all mixed up together. Everything was everywhere.

A wind blew through us. All was still around us as we swirled like smoke.

***

I woke up in a panic. I had been dreaming about spinning in circles. That's all I could remember, just spinning faster and faster.

The room was bright and for a moment I couldn't remember where I was. I pushed myself up onto my elbows.

"Mmm," said Lilith, half-asleep beside me. She mumbled something I didn't understand.

My head pulsed sickly with each heartbeat. I swung my legs over the side of the bed and stood up. The room tilted like a boat. I had to steady myself on the bed frame until the dizziness passed.

"What are you doing?" said Lilith.

"Looking for my clothes," I said.

Lilith sat up, rubbing her eyes. "Why?" she said.

"I have to get back," I said. "I need to go back home."

"Why? What's wrong?"

"Nothing. I just need to get back home."

"Don't go," she said. "Come here, come lie down with me."

"I can't," I said. "I have work tomorrow. Or today? I don't know what day it is. I might already be late for work, I don't know."

"You said you hate work," she said.

"I do. But I need to do it."

"Why? For food? You can get food here. You can get all the food you want here. Why go back to do something you hate?"

"Well," I said, "I mean, I can't just..."

"Look at me," said Lilith.

She was sitting up in bed, propped up on her

19

elbows.

"I'll lose my job," I said. "And then I won't be able to pay rent, and if I don't pay rent, I'll lose my apartment…"

"You can stay here," said Lilith. "You don't have to pay for rent here, or food. Do you miss your job? Do you wish you were in your apartment right now? What will you do when you're there?"

I thought about it. "Nothing," I said. "Get drunk by myself, probably."

"You can get drunk here," she said. "With me."

"That does sound better," I said.

She smiled for moment, then she looked sad. "Don't go back," she said.

I looked down at my little pile of clothes, then back at her. I climbed back into bed and sat next to her. She wrapped her arms around my neck and rested her head on my shoulder.

"Don't go," she said quietly.

I wrapped my arm around her shoulders and squeezed her against me.

She was asleep again soon, breathing slowly.

I ran my fingers through her hair and stared at the black box on the ceiling.

***

Later, we sat out on the street. I was drinking a beer, trying to get the alkaline taste of the Milk out of my mouth and calm the buzzing in my head. Everything was too bright and clear under the glowing sunless dome of the sky. I felt like a stripped wire.

"How do I know this isn't all a dream?" I said. There were buildings on our side of the street, but the other side just dropped off into a ravine of pale sand and broken glass. Past the sparkling sand a ways off, there were more buildings, half built.

"I feel that sometimes," said Lilith. "I think

because of the Milk. Of course, who can ever be sure?" She smiled at me, knees pulled up against her chest, arms around her legs. "And what would be the difference?"

"Well," I said. "If this is a dream, then I'm the only one who's real. And that would mean you aren't real, which would suck."

She laughed. "In a dream, your mind makes all of the things. A mind pretends there is a world and pretends there are people and pretends to be one of the people."

I took another sip of my beer, but the bitter taste lingered in the back of my throat. "Are you saying that if it's a dream, it might be your dream instead of mine?"

"I am saying," she said, "both of us would be part of the same mind, equally. Both of us, everyone in the dream, would be equally real. Or not real."

I finished the beer and tossed it into the ravine, squinting to follow its arc to the ground. A small robot crawled out of the sand and grabbed the bottle and scurried away. "Then I wish this was a dream," I said, "so we could really be together, as one mind. How can two people ever be together if they're still two different minds?"

"Come on," she grabbed my hand and pulled me to my feet, "you think too much. Don't get lost in your head. Let's walk around."

The streets were mostly deserted, as usual. We saw few people in the distance. You could see long wires coming up from their heads, extending way up into the sky.

"Where do all the wires go?" I asked.

"The computer," Lilith said, "same as the ones from the black boxes. Blue wires always go to the computer. They have headphones with blue wires."

"Why don't you have headphones like that? It

seems like most people around here do."

She shrugged. She was looking up at me with her grey, slitted eyes. I saw her lips gain a hint of a smile from the eye contact. "I don't know," she said, "I don't like being told what to do. The headphones are for the computer to tell you what to do."

"But you can just take them off if you want?" I said. "The computer doesn't get mad? Send angry robots after you or anything?"

She laughed. "No," she said. "The computer loves us. It doesn't get mad. We can do what we want to. It loves us. That's what you do when you love something."

She touched my hand with her fingers. Her finger tips felt like tiny hard spheres against my skin. The buzzing behind my eyes was getting worse. "Then why does it give people headphones to wear at all?" I said.

"For the people who want to be told what to do. People don't know what to do. They like being told."

She leaned her head against my shoulder as we walked, and I felt a warm happy feeling inside, but outside I felt stripped and raw. Every nerve felt stripped.

***

We needed more Milk so we went to see the Olm.

The first time I met the Olm, he terrified me. Now he mainly just annoyed me.

"Back already?" he said when we came in. We met him in the basement of a building that looked like every other half-finished building. His skin was a wet pink that glistened under a single overhead lamp and he was wearing a shapeless tan overcoat, just like the first time we met him. His head was flat with an elongated snout, like a pink salamander, and he didn't have any eyes.

"Aren't you happy to see us?" I said.

He laughed again.

Lilith poked me and gave me an annoyed look. "Yes could we have another of the same please?" she said.

"You sure?" said the Olm. "You don't want to upgrade to a bigger volume? Or do you just like coming back to see my pretty face?" His tongue flashed out and licked the smooth, empty surface of his head.

"I only have three money left," Lilith said.

The room was small and damp-smelling, though I couldn't actually see the edges beyond the yellow circle of light from the lamp. It sounded small.

"Only three?" the Olm reached into his overcoat and pulled out a glass vial, about three times the size of the last one. "Only three money. Of course, there are other ways to pay, sweetness."

"Just the same as last time, please," I said.

"Right, right," he said, his smooth pink hand sliding back under his overcoat and coming out with another tiny vial. "The customer is always right, of course. Three will still be a great deal. For anyone else, three wouldn't be enough for shit. But for my favorite customer? And her... friend? Of course."

She placed the three tiny yellow bills in his hand and he gave her the vial. "Thank you so much," she said. "I am sorry we came without very much notice. We are too busy having fun, I guess." She laughed, holding the vial up to the light. Pure, opaque white.

"Of course," he said. "Anytime. Anything for you, sweetness, you know."

"Yeah, thanks," I said. I took Lilith's empty hand. The chair scraped across the cement floor as I stood and I felt the sound scrape across the surface of my brain. "Thank you so much."

"We don't get too many of you down here," said

the Olm, his head tilted towards me now. "People from one level up, I mean. It's nice. It's nice having you people down here, when it happens."

"What, do we smell different?" I said.

His tongue flicked out into the empty air. "Something like that," he said. He tilted towards Lilith, raising his hand and making a gesture with it like a talking mouth that I guess was supposed to be a wave. "Bye, sweetness." His hands were too small. He was the size of a man, at least six feet I would guess if he were standing up, but his hands were like a baby's. They looked like the hands of a fetus, really, since they were shiny and pink too.

***

Out on the street, Lilith walked looking down at the vial in her palm and I walked next to her.

"We don't have to buy shit from that thing, you know," I said. "I know where we can find a river of that stuff. A fucking ocean."

She laughed.

"Seriously!" I said. "There's like a gigantic fucking lake of the stuff, in the caves between the surface, where I come from, and here. No joke."

"Really?" she said.

"Yeah! I mean, it's got to be the same stuff. A whole lake of it! We could just take a jar up there and fill it up. I bet you anything it's the same stuff. We could get as much as we want. We could have enough for ourselves and sell the extra. I am not fucking joking."

"A whole lake?" she said.

"At least a lake."

She turned and put the palm of her hand to my chest to stop me. She held the vial between two fingers. "Kneel down," she said. "Stick out your tongue."

***

I was lying on the bed, staring at that black box on the ceiling with the blue wire.

"It's weird how it never gets dark here," I said.

"Not so weird to me," said Lilith. She was lying next to me, resting her head on my chest. "Thump... thump..." she said. "It goes faster when you breathe in and then slower when you breathe out."

I felt her eyelashes.

"The heart beat is a weird thing," she said. "It goes all the time. All the time, even when you sleep! But there's a space between the beats. There's one beat, then there is a space, then there is another beat. The beats are very short, but the space is long. When you add it up, most of our life is spent in the space between, when our heart isn't beating at all."

"That is weird," I said. "Now all I can think about is my heart beating. Don't talk about it, it makes me think about it. And then I think about breathing and suddenly I'm in control of my breathing and it's annoying."

She laughed. "You don't have to control it. It won't stop if you don't control it. It never stops."

"Well, except when you die."

"What do you mean?" she said.

I stared at the ceiling. It was plain white, but I could see the texture. It seemed to swirl, but every time a focused on one spot it was still. "I kind of like that it's always light out," I said, "but it's messing with my sleep schedule, that's for sure."

She lifted her head off my chest and pushed herself up on one elbow, bringing her face up next to mine. "What do you mean, 'when you die'?" she said. "You aren't going to die."

"Well, not right now..."

"Why would you do anything to make you die?"

I turned to look at her. She looked annoyed.

"I wouldn't do anything like that," I said.

"Then why would you say 'when you die'? Don't say that."

I opened my mouth to say something, then stopped. We stared at each other and then she looked really sad for a second and instantly like a shock I felt it, a sharp stab down my throat into my stomach. Then her arms were around me and she was squeezing me.

"You won't die," she head. Her face was pressed against my neck. "The computer loves us. It doesn't want us to die. It wouldn't have made us just to die."

I squeezed her back and didn't say anything. She slowly relaxed.

She took my hand and pressed it against my own chest.

"See?" She said. "It's doing it all the time. Thump… Thump…"

"Do you think the computer made the above-ground world too?" I said. "Where I came from?"

"How else would it be there?"

"Well, I don't know. I always thought that people like me built the cities. But I don't know, now that I've seen all this down here, I don't know what to think. Maybe it's all a trick. Maybe the computer made all of it and put us there with false memories or something. Like a science experiment."

"It doesn't trick," she said. "It must not have made where you come from or it would watch you like it watches us. Most people have the headphones to tell them what to do. People don't have the head phones up there?"

"Not like that, no," I said. "No one tells people what to do up there except other people. Maybe it made us and then left us to come down here. People feel abandoned a lot, they have a bunch of religions about it, trying to explain it. I think some people would really like it if they had a computer telling them what to do all the time. It's hard trying to figure out what to do by yourself, with no one giving you instructions."

"It is hard sometimes," she said. "But I still like it more."

"Yeah, me too, I guess."

We were quiet for a moment. It was strange how the light never moved on the ceiling. Sometimes it almost felt like time wasn't moving at all.

"I think people feel abandoned because when you're a baby, everything's taken care of for you," I said. "Then as you get older, you have more and more responsibilities until finally you're responsible for everything, and then suddenly everything's stressful and you have to worry about things. And we all sort of remember a time when we didn't have to worry and we all kind of wish we could go back to that. Down here, you don't have to worry. You get free food from the food stations. You don't have to pay rent. You'll never need anything down here, everything's taken care of."

"That's true." She was resting her head on my chest again. "Faster... and slower," she said. "Faster... and slower."

It wasn't too much longer before we ran out of Milk again.

Part 2

Lucas and I were sitting on the roof of some night club at a table under a heat lamp. We had relocated to the roof after we'd gotten sick of trying to yell at each other over the music. Up here the music was reduced to a muffled thudding.

This was back up on the surface, a few weeks later.

"Why did you want to meet here anyway?" I said.

Lucas shrugged. "I don't know," he said. "Isn't this the kind of place where people make drug deals? It seems like that's what you see in the movies."

"That doesn't mean we have to do it."

Lucas laughed. "I don't know, I'm pretty sure it does mean that. Besides, it's always interesting to see what the hip, young people are into. Notice how shiny everything is in there? People haven't really evolved much beyond birds when it comes to liking shiny things, have we? And if you need more proof, look no further than the nearest douchebag's preposterously expensive wristwatch. And the music! A never ending four-on-the-floor beat with auto-tuned hooks thrown on top of it. Mass-produced, assembly line stuff, digitally polished to a lustrous sheen, as slick and shiny as any surface in that club. Truly, it is the perfect soundtrack to the times we live in."

"I think you're putting too much thought into this," I said. "We could have just gone to a place where we'd be able to talk to each other without yelling and didn't have to pay a cover charge to get in."

Lucas laughed again, brushing the hair out of his eyes. "Always the pragmatist. Can't argue with that. Next time we'll go someplace sleazier to do this. I'll find us the dive-iest dive bar in town. That may be the better aesthetic for a drug deal anyway. Though I guess it depends on the drug. A place like this would be perfect for cocaine, for example, but not, on the other hand, crack cocaine. I guess the real question is, this Milk stuff: is it a high-class drug or a low-class drug?"

"I don't know," I said. "So far you, me, and whoever you sell the stuff to are the only people who do it."

"And of course, Lilith," he smiled. "Don't forget her."

"Yeah," I said.

"So a highly exclusive drug then, isn't it? One could consider that high-class. If you ignore the fact that between us we own very few yachts."

Someone on the other side of the roof yelled "Woo!" and tripped over a chair. People laughed and yelled "party foul" at him.

"Well here it is," I said. I slid him a paper bag across the table. Inside were five vials of Milk wrapped in a rubber band.

"Well so much for class!" he said. "For an establishment like this I would expect at least a black briefcase with shiny metal combination locks! For Christ's sake, man, the aesthetics!" He slid me a different paper bag. "I included a special treat, just for you."

I looked in the bag. There was a roll of bills and a small bag of weed.

"Well look who it is," said Lucas. Lilith leaned down and wrapped her arms around my neck from behind me, pressing her face against mine.

"Hello hello," she said. Her breath smelled like Milk and vodka. She was damp with sweat.

"How is it in there?" I said. "Having fun?"

"I am having fun!" said Lilith. "The music is fun. It's so loud and there are so many moving lights and colors! I can feel the sound in my chest. It feels so good to move in rhythm." She laughed. "People I don't know give me free alcohol."

"Mostly the male people, I'm guessing," said Lucas, smiling up at her. You could mistake him for a twelve-year-old if it weren't for the dark circles under his eyes.

"See, I told you you'd like it," I said.

"You should come inside and dance with me," she said. She rubbed her face against mine like a cat.

I laughed. "I don't know about that. Dancing isn't really my thing. Unless I get really, really drunk."

"Then get really, really drunk," she said.

"Getting really drunk while carrying a bag of money and illegal drugs around isn't really a good idea," I said.

"And that, my dear, is the benefit of carrying a bag full of drugs that aren't illegal yet," said Lucas. He tucked the paper bag into an inner coat pocket. "I, for one, am up for a little partying, Lilith. Come take a shot with me."

"Bleh more vodka," said Lilith, sticking out her tongue.

"Don't worry, free vodka tastes better. Or haven't you noticed?" said Lucas, pushing his chair back and standing up. "Come now, into the shiny, pounding abyss!"

I sighed. "Could you bring me one when you come back out?" I said.

"That's more like it!" said Lucas. "One little drink won't kill you."

Lilith stood up and turned to follow him. I touched her arm and she turned back.

"We do have to leave soon, though," I said. "Ok?"

"Ok," she said. She smiled at me and headed back into the club.

***

We left the club after what felt like forever and headed to the subway station.

Lilith held onto my arm for support, struggling to keep her balance as if the ground were made of jello.

"Oh!" she said, pointing her finger at something, tugging on my arm, trying to drag me towards a nearby telephone pole. I tilted my weight against her but she dragged me sideways as we walked. "What is this? Why are these papers here?"

There was a flyer stapled to the telephone pole on top of a tangled mass of half-ripped old flyers and staples. It had a stylized drawing of a cat shooting laser beams out of its eyes, with a large date and a list of band names and set times. The cat's head was bisected and opened like a medical diagram, but it was drawn cheerfully so it didn't seem to upset about it. A cartoonish zigzag of energy traced back along its optic nerve and into the multicolored wrinkles of its brain.

"Looks like a flyer for a show," I said.

Lilith tugged on my arm. I sighed and stopped resisting her pulling, letting her drag me over to the telephone pole.

"A show?" she said.

"Like, a concert," I said. "Live music."

"Music? Like what we were just hearing? Very loud thumping sounds?"

"Sort of like what they were playing the club, yeah," I said. "And definitely just as loud. Probably louder. But with actual bands instead of a DJ. Like, people playing the actual instruments on stage."

Lilith gasped. "Oh!" she said. "Playing instruments? I want to see!" She leaned in closer to the flier. "Black Bar?" she said. "What is that?"

"The name of the venue, probably," I said.

"Can we go to Black Bar and see this?" she said.

"Maybe," I said tugging on her hand, trying to pull her away from the pole.

She looked up at me, her brow furrowed. "You sound like you don't want to go," she said.

I sighed. "I said maybe we can go, ok? I'm just tired and I want to go home. Can we keep walking in the direction of the train station? Please?"

Lilith flinched and I looked away. I tugged on her hand and started walking again, pulling her behind me.

We walked in silence for about a block.

"We can look up this Black Bar place tomorrow," I said. "And see when the show is and what kind of music it is and everything. Ok?"

She didn't answer me.

"Ok?" I said. "Sounds good?"

"Ok," she said.

***

On the train home, Lilith rested her head on my shoulder and dozed off almost immediately.

In the seat across from us was a discarded newspaper with a large-print headline: "Missing child count continues to grow." Below that was a row of children's photos.

Further down in the subway car, a man resting his head against the window began to throw up in his sleep. Luckily we only had a few more stops. My head was starting to hurt. I wanted more Milk, but I realized I should probably just go to sleep when I got home and wait until tomorrow.

Just before our stop, I shook Lilith to wake her up. She stirred. Half-asleep, she started to kiss my neck.

"Faster and slower," she murmured. She opened her mouth and I felt the sharp points of her teeth scrape across my skin.

"Wake up, Lilith," I said, "we have to get off here. Wake up."

***

Lucas was a small-time drug dealer. I was used to buying weed from him, so when Lilith and I decided to come up to the surface to sell Milk, it made sense to go through him. I didn't know anything about selling drugs to people, so I figured it would be easier to just sell it to him in bulk and let him sort out the details. We would give him the pure liquid and he would dilute it and soak blotter paper in it to sell in little squares.

The giant pool of Milk in the cave wasn't exactly the same as what we were buying from the Olm. It was much more mild. A few drops of the Olm's product were enough to have a decent quality trip, but small quantities of the cave stuff didn't seem to do anything at all. Finally Lilith just scooped up a handful and drank it. A few minutes later, she started throwing up. A few minutes after that, her pupils were huge and she was laughing uncontrollably.

She was holding her hands up to the light of the lamp we'd brought. "It's definitely working," she said. She laughed. "It's like they're hollow, broken shells. The shadow parts are just empty." Then she rolled over onto her side and choked out a thin stream of bile, clutching her stomach, her knees drawn up to her chest, retching even though there was nothing left in her stomach. She was drenched in sweat and shivering.

I crouched next to her in the dark. I didn't know what to do. I didn't know if I could carry her to the boat and get her all the way to the surface and get her to a hospital. I didn't know if I could take back down to the lower level and find some robots to help her. Did they have medical robots down there? We'd never had to look for any before.

She kept telling me she would be ok. I crouched next to her and did nothing, not because I trusted her word but because I was too terrified to do anything. I don't know how long it took, but slowly she got better. The dry heaves stopped, then the shivering. Finally, she sat up and touched my arm with a cold, damp hand.

"This is what we want," she said, "we just need to fix it." She squeezed my arm. "There's so much!"

We found out through trial and error that by running the liquid through a water filter and boiling it we could make a concentrated version that didn't make us sick, basically the same as the Olm's, though maybe with a slightly worse hang-over.

Since the underground city was mostly empty, we decided to sell it on the surface. Also we wouldn't have to compete with the Olm that way. So we hauled up some jugs of the stuff and prepared it in my apartment. Then I got in contact with Lucas.

He tried the Milk and loved it. He said it was the best chemical hallucinogen he'd ever tried. So we came up with a business arrangement.

***

Smoking weed while on Milk made time slow and disjointed. I was lying on the bed watching Lilith put on makeup.

"I don't know why you do that," I said.

She was standing in front of the full-length mirror on the closet door. Her reflection looked at me for a second, then back to herself. "I like makeup," she said.

"I like the way you look without makeup."

"People don't look pale like that up here," she said.

"I like pale."

She didn't say anything. I tried to come up with a way to say she looked pretty, but I couldn't think of how to phrase it. Everything I thought of seemed awkward. You look pretty. You look beautiful. Everything felt forced. People say stuff like that in movies. Do people actually say stuff like that in real life? Does it just come naturally to them?

"It's not like I go all goth when I'm down in your section," I said, but she didn't get the reference.

She was doing something to her eyelids with a pencil now. It looked dangerous to me.

"What are you going to go do?" I said. "When you're out. You know… on the town. Out on the town."

"I am going to go look at some pretty clothes to buy," she said.

"Shopping," I said.

"Yes," she said.

"Should I go with you? Do you want me to come?"

"It's not fun to go shopping with you," she said.

I laughed. "That's because I hate it," I said. "I understand that this stuff is new and fun for you, but I've been living in this place my whole life. I'm sick of it. I'm sick of… shopping and buying things. That's all people do up here is buy things. Work all day and then buy things."

"We don't have to work," she said.

"I know. And believe me, I am very happy about that. But still, though. It's all bullshit. They make all these ads convincing you that you need more stuff, you always need more stuff, you won't be happy until you have more stuff. So then people go out and buy it. But they don't really need to buy more stuff, they don't need more stuff."

"I like shopping," she said. "I think it's fun, and I earn half of the money. I pay for half of the rent, I pay for food, I can do what I want to have fun."

I opened my mouth to say something, but my thoughts had scattered like birds.

"What do you want me to do to have fun?" she said. "We can do something together if you want, other than go shopping. What do you want to do instead?"

"Uhh… Stay home and do drugs?" I said. "And eat

snack foods and not do anything? Yeah, ok, I suck at having fun."

She was done putting on makeup. She was gathering things up and putting them in her purse.

"We should go back underground, Lilith. Everything down there is weird and clean and new. It's like a dream."

"For you," she said, putting her jacket on. "I have spent my whole life down there, remember?"

She was standing at the bedroom door, with her hand on the knob, where she had stopped and turned on her way out. Her jacket was white wool, with large white buttons. Her pants were white, her blouse sky-blue, with a thin silver necklace draped across her collar bone.

"You look really nice," I said. "How can someone who's spent their whole life never shopping for clothes be so fashionable?"

The corner of her mouth curled up in a smile and her face seemed to soften. She took her hand from the doorknob and came over to the side of the bed. She leaned over and kissed me. The touch yanked me suddenly into the moment, but I wasn't sure where else I had been.

And then she was back at the door and I was wiping her lipstick off me.

"Don't do that!" she said.

"Then don't put weird stuff on your lips!" I said.

She laughed. She opened the door. "We'll go back down again soon. Ok? At least to visit."

She stood there and looked at me for a long time that can't have been more than a second or two and then I was sitting in an empty room.

***

I woke up on the bed later that afternoon and at first I wasn't sure why. I didn't remember falling asleep. I sat up, still in a haze, and looked around. The TV was on mute. There was a news story on, cycling through family photos of various adults and children. The text on the bottom of the screen read "Still Missing."

Then the doorbell rang and I realized that was the sound that had woken me up. I climbed out of bed and stumbled into the living area of the apartment, closing the bedroom door behind me. I looked through the peephole of the front door. There was nobody there. I made a small opening in the blinds next to the door and looked through to see two small children in business suits standing at the door.

I stood there for a moment, trying to process this, until they rang the doorbell again and I opened the door.

"Good afternoon, sir," said the slightly taller child. "Have you heard news of the coming end of days?"

"Which one?" I said.

The shorter child held out a pamphlet and I took it from him. The cover was an illustration of a burning city collapsing into a giant crack in the earth. The heading read: "Are YOU prepared?"

"The Reverend Timmy first predicted the coming apocalypse a year ago," said the taller child. He turned to the smaller child.

"'And the Earth shall be torn asunder,'" the smaller child read from a pamphlet identical to the one he'd handed me. "'And fire and death shall rise from below. And all of mankind yet on the Earth shall be killed.'"

"Since making this prediction," said the taller child,

"the Reverend Timmy has been working tirelessly to save mankind."

"'And so he conceived of the New Equipment,'" read the smaller child his stilted manner, "'and he did begin to build it. And recruit others for this purpose, that it may be built. Only through the New Equipment can mankind be saved. And yet only he with the purity of a child may through the New Equipment pass.'" He turned over his pamphlet to show me an illustration of a giant, tangled jungle gym reaching up into the clouds and disappearing into a glowing portal of light.

"Do you have any children, sir?" said the taller child.

I shook my head no.

He nodded solemnly. "I understand that this may come as troubling news," he said, "that only the children may escape the apocalypse. In fact, you may be wondering why I would bother to tell you, an adult, about any of this if your fate were inevitable. Until recently, in fact, to do so would have been futile and even cruel. However…" He turned again to his companion.

"'And thus was the Reverend Timmy blessed with the power to transmute the human form, and change man into child, and in so doing, allow him to escape the great sundering of the earth and climb the New Equipment into Heaven, so that all of mankind might be saved.'"

"I realize this may be difficult to believe, but I assure you, it is true. In fact," said the taller child, "I myself was once an adult, as you are."

He held out a photo of an adult that looked a fair amount like him.

"But the Reverend Timmy blessed me and took me below the Earth and there I was reborn," said the taller child, his eyes glazing over with reverence, "As you could be, sir, if you but choose to see the truth and choose to save yourself from the fiery pits of Hell that will, in but a few short months, swallow the Earth."

The two watched me, waiting for a response.

"I'll think about it," I said, starting to close the door.

"Of course, of course," said the taller child, pushing in front of the other to stay in my narrowing doorway. "Should you decide to choose salvation, simply call the number on the back of your pamphlet and—"

"Thanks," I said and pushed the door shut.

I tossed the pamphlet onto the coffee table and went back to the bedroom to smoke another bowl.

***

"My whole life, art was the only the thing that made living seem worthwhile," Lucas said. "When you're inundated with art from a young age, cartoons, movies, music, from a young age, real life ends up seeming really dull by comparison. I mean, for Christ's sake, children's movies are the worst. They're filled with adventure and amazement and in the end the hero gets some beautiful woman and they live happily ever after. And what is real life compared to that? Real life is boring and humiliating and you never get what you want. It's shit, really."

I was in the kitchen, trying to pour Milk from a pot into a plastic water bottle through a funnel. It should have been simple enough, but it was made more difficult by the haze of weed and Milk and alcohol. Sometimes you don't realize how fucked up you actually are until you try to do something carefully. Lucas was sitting next to Lilith on the couch in the living room.

"So since all the art I was exposed to brought so much joy to my young life," Lucas said, "I decided early on that I wanted to be an artist. I wanted to bring that kind of joy to others." He leaned back on the couch, running his hands through his hair, putting the side of one foot up on his knee. Lilith was watching his face as he talked. "It wasn't until much later, after spending two years of my life and a large amount of money I didn't actually have at some fucking art school, that I realized that fucking everybody wants to be an artist. I thought I could provide the world with a service, this special gift of 'art' that would enrich the lives of others. But not only is there plenty of art in the world already, there's actually way too much. We are drowning in art because of assholes like me. Millions of assholes like me who thought that they were actually helping people with their mediocre art."

Finally, I had emptied the whole pot. The water bottle was about two-thirds full with thick white liquid. A few drops would be enough to send you on a trip for hours. It was a ridiculously large amount.

"At a certain point," said Lucas, "after god only knows how many bands and magazines and art collectives I tried to start, I finally realized how pointless and redundant I was. If art was water, humanity was drowning and I was trying to save a drowning man by spraying him in the face with a hose." He sat up suddenly, uncrossing his legs and gesturing with his hands. "And not only that, but I realized that art was actually a trick! It tricked people with boring, shitty jobs into thinking that their lives were actually rich and full and interesting. It let them pretend that they weren't basically slaves, doing repetitive activities that they don't care about every day of their lives just so they can pay the bills. So not only is art redundant, you could argue that it's actually evil. It keeps the slaves just complacent enough to keep the whole shitty system going." He sat back in the couch again and smiled. "And that's why I became a drug dealer instead."

Lilith laughed, leaning over and touching his arm. "I don't see too much difference," she said. "Drugs make people happy too, like art."

"That's true, I guess," said Lucas. "Sort of. I don't know, it seems more honest though."

"You just try to help people," said Lilith. Her hand was still resting on his arm.

"I know," said Lucas, "I'm a fucking hero, I know." She laughed.

I screwed the cap onto the water bottle.

"And you are good to go," I said.

"Excellent," said Lucas. "Most good."

He stood up and walked into the kitchen to take the bottle from me. "Now THAT is what I am talking about," he said. He reached into his pocket and pulled out a large role of bills wrapped in a rubber band and handed it to me.

"It has been a pleasure, as always," he said. He shook my hand and gave Lilith an awkward invisible hat-tip. "But I must be off on my merry way. I will be seeing you."

"See you," said Lilith.

Lucas tucked the bottle into his backpack and left.

I put the empty pot into the sink and filled it with water. Lilith sat on the couch, striped by the light coming through the blinds. I opened the freezer and took out a frosted bottle of vodka and poured myself a shot. I leaned back on the counter, holding the cold shot glass, and watched Lilith get up from the couch and go into the bedroom and close the door behind her.

I took the shot. I set down the glass and walked unsteadily into the living room. I sat down on the couch and turned on the TV.

***

I watched a documentary about cheetahs. It was about a mother cheetah and her two cubs trying to find food. When the mother cheetah finally managed to kill a gazelle, hyenas showed up to attack her and steal the dead gazelle. The mother slowly bled to death from hyena bites. Then the cubs headed off on their own to find food. They couldn't find any food, so they starved to death. That was the end of the documentary. Up next was a show about people finding out what their antiques were really worth. One guy was really excited about this wooden desk he had that he thought would be worth a lot of money, but it turned out it was a fake. He was really disappointed.

Sometime later, during a different show where puppets were singing a song about tolerance, the doorbell rang.

I stood up and almost fell over. I had been sitting down for so long I hadn't realized how drunk I actually was. The vodka bottle was warm now, sitting on the coffee table in a pool of condensation. I made my way over to the door. I felt like I was walking on a boat.

I opened the door to reveal two little kids in business suits.

"Good afternoon, sir," one of them began. He was unenthusiastic. "Have you heard news of the coming end of days?"

"Uh some kids like you guys were already over here the other day," I said. "I still have the thing, the pamphlet…"

"Holy shit!" said the child, suddenly full of energy. "It's you!"

"I… what?"

"Jordan! It's me, Tom!" said the child.

I stared at him. "What Tom?"

"Dude, don't fucking act like this," said the child. "Tom. Your co-worker Tom. You're Jordan, right?"

"Yeah," I said.

"Tom, dude! We cleaned up dead bodies together?"

"What the hell are you…" and then I recognized him. It was Tom as a little kid. He was a little kid, but it was definitely Tom. He smiled, recognizing that I finally recognized him.

"Dude, this is fucking crazy. I mean, obviously lots of what's happened recently has been fucking crazy. But still! Random." He turned to his slightly shorter companion. "Listen, you go on back to headquarters. Or keep going on the route by yourself. Whatever. This is my friend, I haven't seen him in forever. We need to catch up." The kid stared at him blankly. "Beat it, ok?" said Tom. "Jesus."

The other kid left and I led the child version of Tom

into the living room.

"Man," he said. "I thought for sure the lizard people must've got you. Or something, man! It's been months! You said you were coming right back up, and then I never heard from you or anything!"

"Yeah," I said. "I got distracted I guess. Want a beer?"

"Shit yeah I do!" said Tom. "Fucking A, I can't believe you're still alive, dude! I'll drink to that!"

***

"That stuff about 'transmuting the human form,' as you can see, that was no fucking joke," Tom was saying. He was sitting on the arm chair, his legs dangling off the edge, taking swigs of his beer.

"I guess not," I said. "So… why? How did you actually get convinced to so something like this?"

"It didn't take too much convincing, man," said Tom. "Apocalypse coming up from under the Earth? It's the goddamn lizard people. I saw that city with my own two eyes. I'm not stupid. These kids, them and this Reverend Timmy kid, they're the only ones offering a way out. The New Equipment? That shit's real too, man. I've seen it. It's epic as hell."

"So you got changed into a kid," I said, "so they'd let you climb up that thing? Just like in the brochure?"

"Yeah, dude," he said. "I'm not going to get eaten and fucked with scaly reptile dicks and all that. No way."

"Tom," I said. "I was down there for a long time, I'm telling you, there aren't any lizard people down there. And besides, where are you going to escape to? Do you honestly believe that tower leads to heaven?"

"First of all," said Tom, "I know for a fact that there are lizard people down there because I met one. He's like a traitor lizard person. I mean, don't get me wrong, he's still creepy and gross but at least he's helping us humans out, giving us the pill. He gave me my pill anyway. Secondly, of course it doesn't lead to 'heaven', dude, but it leads somewhere. Think about it: hollow earth. What makes you think we're actually on the surface right now? We're already a layer down, man! We're probably like a buffer layer to help keep the lizards out, or at least slow them down. The New Equipment doesn't lead to 'heaven' it leads to the real surface!"

"You met a lizard person?" I said. "He gave you a pill? What are you talking about?"

"Yeah, dude. He's fucking horrifying. But, like I said, he's helping us out, helping us escape. He's one of the good guys."

"What does he look like?" I said.

"He's basically like a person, except he has a snout. You know, like a lizard-shaped head. He's all pink and shiny and he has no eyes."

I felt something twist in my stomach. "The Olm," I said.

"Yeah! So wait, you met him too?"

"Yeah, I did," I said. "He's not a good guy. He's an asshole. And he's not a lizard, he's more like a salamander."

"Lizard people, salamander people, so what? What do you mean he's not a good guy?"

"I mean, he's fucking shady. We used to buy drugs from him. He's not a good guy."

"Wait, who's 'we'?" said Tom.

"And how could this not be the surface? I don't get what you're trying to tell me."

"I'm telling you, dude, we're a lizard buffer."

My heart was racing. Panic was sobering me up like a slap to the face. And I didn't even know what exactly I was afraid of. I didn't understand enough to know what I should be afraid of, but I was afraid.

"None of this makes any sense," I repeated.

"What's going on?" said Lilith. She was standing in the bedroom door in her pajamas. "Who are you arguing?"

Tom leapt out of the chair. "Oh fuck!" he said. He backed towards the door, tripping over his tiny feet, holding his beer bottle in front of him like a weapon.

"Why is this child here?" said Lilith. "What's going on?"

"What the fuck," said Tom, "is a fucking lizard person doing in your house?"

"What?" I said. "This is Lilith."

"I don't care what its name is, for Christ's sake, kill it!" Tom's voice was becoming increasingly shrill.

Lilith crossed her arms and glared. "Who are you to talk like that?" she said. "Jordan, why is this child in our apartment?"

"Ok look, everyone calm down," I said. "Tom. This is Lilith. She's my friend. And she's not a lizard. Look at her. She's a human."

"Bullshit," said Tom. "She's in disguise, man. That's how they infiltrate human government and shit. They disguise themselves as humans. Look at her eyes, man! Look at her fucking teeth!"

"So what you're saying is," I said, "is that these lizard people can disguise themselves as humans. They can turn you from a grown man into a child, no problem. But they fucked up the eyes and teeth? They couldn't do the eyes and teeth right? They could copy every other part of the human anatomy in perfect detail but they couldn't do the fucking eyes and teeth right?"

Tom opened his mouth to say something but couldn't seem to form words.

"Tom," I said. "Lilith is my friend. If you are my friend, respect me enough to listen to what I say. Calm the fuck down, Tom. There are no goddamn lizard people."

Tom continued to eye Lilith suspiciously, but he moved back to the arm chair. He climbed back up into it very carefully, to avoid spilling his beer.

Lilith was staring at me, arms still crossed. "Jordan," she said. "Please tell me. Who is this?"

***

"I don't know how to explain," she said. "I don't know very much, to be honest. I know the computer made me. The computer made the city and the robots and all of the people."

We were all sitting in the living room, talking. Tom had calmed down a bit but he was still fidgety and his face was twitchy and nervous.

"Why though?" said Tom. "Why did it make all that?"

Lilith turned up her palms. "Why were you made?" she said. "The computer loves us. It made us so we could be alive and so we could be happy. The robots are still building the city. It is a new city. I am new also.

There were not very many people before I was made, I think. I was made in a plastic tube. The robots showed us the tubes when we were in class when we were very young. We saw new people growing in the tubes and they told us that we came from the same place. The robots took care of us and taught us about languages and math and everything. They explained how the computer loved us. When we got old enough, they gave us places to live and left us to take care of ourselves. They left headphones for us, if we wanted, that tell you what to do. I used my headphones for a while, but then I stopped. I don't want to be told what to do. So I stopped using them, and went out to learn on my own. I learned about the Milk. I learned about money. Food comes free from machines and there is no rent like there is here, the money is only for buying Milk and alcohol, things like that. I found interesting things I could trade for money in construction areas and I used the money to buy Milk and alcohol for fun. I found a music-making box, and sometimes I played that on the street and people would give me money for that." She looked back and forth between me and Tom, chewing on her lower lip. "I don't know what else I can say about it."

Tom eyed her sideways, rubbing his small hands together. "I see," he said.

"I met her on the street the day that you and I went down there," I said. "I found out she spoke English, so I asked her about the city and asked her to show me around. She showed me the Milk and I just got completely lost in that world down there."

There was a moment of quiet. Lilith was sitting next to me on the couch and Tom was sitting on the arm chair, swinging his legs.

"Ok," he said. "I have to say, I am very confused. This whole thing has been a massive mind-fuck from the get go, and I gotta say, our poor minds have been provided with very little lube. But!" he turned to Lilith. "Whatever's going on, you seem chill, I guess. I don't feel like you're on the verge of drinking my spinal fluid or whatever. So I'm sorry I was yelling at you and telling Jordan to kill you and stuff earlier."

Lilith smiled politely at him.

"Man," said Tom. "This is all so crazy. Though I guess that's nothing new," he gestured down at his child's body. "Well, shit, I need to be getting back to the headquarters building or the kids will start wondering where I am. Let me give you guys my phone number, in case you want to get a hold of me or whatever."

After Tom left, Lilith and I sat on the couch quietly for a few moments.

"Do you think that's true?" said Lilith. "That there's another world above this one?"

"I don't know," I said. "At this point I wouldn't be surprised."

We sat quietly for a few more moments. I put my arm around her. She gave me a small, sideways hug and stood up.

"I need to get ready," she said. "I'm going out."

"Going out where?" I said. "With Lucas?"

"Yes, with Lucas," she said. She was walking towards the bedroom. I twisted around over to look watch her go over the back of the couch.

"What are you guys going to do?" I said.

She stopped and turned her face halfway

towards me, looking down and to the side.

"Echobombing," she said.

"Echobombing? What does that mean?"

She sighed. "It's just..." she turned to face me, crossing her arms. "You go out to some clubs and set up these small microphones, hidden around the room. And then Lucas does something and the music goes away and instead the microphone sound comes out of the speakers."

"Oh," I said. "Why?"

"It plays back the sound of the room and it echoes more and more because the microphones pick it up again," said Lilith. "People get confused."

"Oh," I said. "Ok. Sounds fun."

"It is fun," she said.

"Well, don't stay out too late," I said, "we need to go get some more raw milk tomorrow."

"Yeah." She closed the bedroom door behind her.

***

I woke up on the couch in a drunken haze. A door slammed.

"What time is it?" I said.

"I don't know," said Lilith from behind me. I heard her set her purse down on the kitchen counter.

I sat up and checked the time on my phone.

"It's 6 am," I said.

"Ok," said Lilith.

I could feel something through the fog of vodka, a tightness in my stomach. My insides were winding up like a spring. I could feel the blood behind my eyes.

I stood up and walked around the couch. Lilith was rummaging through her purse for something.

"You're just coming home," I said, "at 6 am."

"What difference is it?" she said, not looking up from her purse.

"We have to go down to get more Milk tomorrow," I said. "Or... today, actually. Because it's fucking six in the morning now."

"That is not a job for two people," she said. "You do this one today, just take two gallons by yourself. I'll do it the next time. It's not very hard." She finally looked up at me. Her eyes narrowed. "What? What is the problem? I'm not a child like your friend, I don't have a bedtime, what is the problem?"

I stared at her, breathing heavily through my nose. My jaw hurt. She stared at me. She turned her palms upward and raised her eyebrows as if to re-ask the question then turned towards the bedroom.

"So how is Lucas anyway?" I said.

"What do you mean?" She said, not looking back.

"I mean," I said, "how is he? Is he better than me?"

She stopped in the bedroom doorway and turned to face me.

"Is he better than me?" I said. "What I mean is, is he better at fucking than I am? Is he better at sex than I am? Does he do a better job of fucking you than I ever did, is what I'm asking you."

She stared at me with cold silver eyes, then headed back towards the front door, reaching for her purse on the counter. I grabbed her arm and pulled hard, turning her back towards me.

"Don't touch me!" she jerked her arm out of my grip.

"Just hang on, one second, just let me say

something, just let me say one thing."

"Say it then! Do not touch me!"

"I get this now. I get this whole thing now. You never cared about me as a person. You never cared. I was just something new and exciting that showed up, a guy from another world. That's all I was, something new for you to have fun with. Me, as a person, that never mattered. And then when we came up here, suddenly there were a million new things and lots of new and interesting people and suddenly I didn't matter anymore. You could just throw me away and move on to the next thing, just like that. You never gave a shit about me, I was just some fucking toy for you and I just wasn't fun anymore."

"Oh yes?" she said. She was holding her purse and backing towards the door. "And what about you? What was I except the first pretty girl you met in my city? The first woman you even met in my city? What about me do you like, what about me 'as a person' do you care about other than the way I look, being pale, my eyes, different from anyone up here? Name one thing you like about me besides how I am exotic, like a rare breed of animal!"

"Wh-what? One thing I like? What are you–" I said, then stopped. I thought for a moment. She stood with her back to the door, her hand on the doorknob behind her. "I like that you took the headphones off," I said, "because you didn't like being told what to do."

She laughed one short, bitter laugh. She stood at the door, breathing ragged breaths. She opened the door slowly and worked her way around the edge, not taking her eyes off me.

"I just want—" I said and stopped.

"You hurt my arm," she said. And then she slammed the door and I heard her run away.

I sat down on the couch. I picked up a roach from the coffee table and tried to light it but my hands were shaking too much. I drank more vodka. I drank until I threw up. In the bathroom I found a bottle of cough syrup. I drank it in several long swallows, pausing, forcing myself to keep it down.

I went back into the living room. I tried to light the roach again, but I couldn't.

***

I woke up on the couch, covered in sweat. My heart was fluttering in a very strange way, beating too fast and too lightly.

I heard a voice say: "I'm dying. I must be dying."

I realized it was my voice.

Everything shifted and I realized I was sitting up and then I was lying face down on the floor. I tried to move my arms to push myself up again.

"It's cough syrup," I said. "You're not dying. It's cough syrup and... alcohol. And..."

I climbed up the arm of the couch and pulled myself up onto my feet. Walking was a strange and alien motion. My ears were ringing. My body felt packed in a thick layer of gauze.

I remembered being upset about Lilith, but I didn't feel upset anymore. I couldn't remember what feeling upset was like, exactly. I felt something, but it was very strange. I felt pretty good, actually. I heard myself laugh. It was as if everything was awful, this whole universe was bad and wrong, but that was ok.

Everything was awful and that was ok. I didn't see why anyone would get upset by it.

"Awful isn't a bad thing," I said. "Necessarily."

I remembered I had to do something.

Milk.

I grabbed an empty gallon bottle and made my way outside. It was sometime in the afternoon. The light was dirty and yellow. I closed the door and navigated the key into the lock with some difficulty and locked it. I made sure it was locked. I set off in the direction of the elevator building. For a minute I was worried I might get lost, but then who cared if I got lost? Who cared if anything?

***

I made it to the dead old man's house and into the cave underneath. As I walked through the tunnels I began to sober up slowly, like I was swimming up from deep waters. My stomach hurt and my chest was tight from the cough syrup. The stale, dusty air was difficult to breathe.

When I reached the shore of the Milk lake, I stopped. I stared into the darkness for a long time. The only sound was the gentle sloshing of the Milk on the shore and a low roar of moving liquid echoing from the cavern's distant walls. I put down the empty gallon jug and climbed into the boat and pulled the lever to activate it.

As the boat pulled me into the darkness, as my head cleared, confusion gave way to self-hatred, crushing down on me like I was being buried. At that moment, there was nothing in the universe I wanted more than a drink. I took a vial of Milk out of my pocket, my own personal vial, and considered taking a drop, but I decided not to. Milk would only sharpen everything, make my thoughts run faster. I wanted the exact opposite of that.

The boat ride seemed to take forever.

Finally, the boat scraped up on the shore and I got out and went to the elevator. Free-fall seemed to take forever too. I'd never had to make this trip by myself before.

The elevator slowed to a stop and the door opened. That same old house again, so similar to the one on the surface. Familiar pale grey light filtered through the ragged sheets of plastic over the windows. The old wooden floor creaked beneath my feet. But something seemed different. It wasn't as quiet as it should have been, there was a sort of murmur or a hum in the background that I couldn't place. I opened the door and the sound came crashing down on me all at once.

The street in front of the house, a street that had been completely deserted only a month ago, was swarming with life. Booths and shops lined the road. People in brightly-colored clothes milled about, interacting with street venders and each other, bartering and making small talk and laughing. The house I had just come out of was the only run-down building on the street, a lone condemned building stretching endlessly up into the sky surrounded by shiny businesses, bars, restaurants and stores, all sporting business signs in some alphabet I didn't recognize.

I came down from the rusted metal landing into the street and began to walk in no particular direction. A tall, slender woman wrapped from neck to foot in shiny orange cloth smiled at me as I passed. Her teeth were too small and there were too many of them. Children wandered past with their faces and hair covered in thick white paint, their matted ponytails decorated with colorful ribbons. A tall man with a long white beard watched me as he passed me, his head swaying gracefully from side to side with his beard trailing after it. A man with a veil over his face was purchasing a kite from a street vendor. He laughed at something the street vendor said and shook his hand. The kite was shaped like a butterfly.

As I reached the intersection, I saw a woman on the street corner. She was wearing three bikini tops down the front of her torso, each one covering a pair of small breasts, lined up on her chest and stomach like the nipples on a dog or a cat.

She turned to me as I approached and said something in a language I couldn't understand.

"I'm sorry?" I said.

She smiled. She had orange/red hair and her eyes were a dark royal blue. "Are you looking or are you paying?" she said.

"Paying?" I said.

She raised her eyebrows and made a sweeping gesture down her body.

I stared at her. Every exposed inch of her body was covered in delicate freckles. "I… don't have any money," I said.

She put on a well-rehearsed pout. "Is this true?" she said, shifting her hips to one side and running her hand down a column of breasts.

I stood there for a moment. Her eyes were already

beginning to scan the crowd behind me for viable customers. I reached into my pocket and pulled out my vial of Milk. "Will this work?" I said.

She tried to keep her expression neutral but her eyes lit up immediately. "One hour," she said.

I shrugged. "Sure."

She snatched the vial from my hand and took me by the arm.

"Follow," she said.

We went into the lobby of a building about a block away. The man at the front counter started saying something in a foreign language, gesturing to a board with of times and rates, but the girl cut him off. She made a hand gesture as she spoke, tapping her middle finger and thumb together and the man nodded and gave us a key.

When we got into the room, she pushed me down onto the bed and climbed on top of me, straddling me with her legs. She took out the vial of milk and held it out to me.

"Want a drop before?" she said.

I smiled and shook my head. "It's all you."

She tilted her head back and stuck out her long, narrow tongue. She gave herself one drop, then another.

"I don't suppose there's any booze around here?" I said. "Any alcohol?"

She didn't seem to hear me. Her head was tilted back, eyes closed, smiling at the taste of Milk on her tongue. She squeezed me with her legs and started to take off her bikinis, starting from the top.

"What do you want to do first?" she said.

I was staring up at the ceiling, at the black box with

the blue wire.

"Anything," I said.

***

When I got back to the surface, it was the middle of the night. I had filled up the gallon container with Milk and hauled it back up the ladder into the dead old man's house.

I took the subway. On the train I saw someone reading a newspaper with the headline "Disappearances Tied to Mystery Cult." The woman reading the newspaper noticed me staring at her and I quickly looked away.

When I got back to the apartment, the light was on. The blinds were down but not completely closed. There was no one in the living room. I opened the door as quietly as I could.

I set the gallon jug down on the kitchen counter. The bedroom door was open just a crack. The light was on in there too. As I got closer I could hear quiet voices.

I walked to the bedroom door, stepping slowly and carefully. Through the small opening by the hinge, I could see Lilith standing with her back to me.

"I miss her," Lilith was saying. "I never saw her again after that."

I put my eye up to the opening. Lilith was standing in front of the closet door. I could see the reflection of the side of her face, looking up. There was an open duffel bag at her feet with clothes in it.

"It wasn't your fault," said Lucas.

In the mirror, I saw her eyes searching his face. She stood up on her tiptoes and kissed him, her hand on his chest. She was holding a white jacket on a coat hanger in her other hand. His long hair blocked her face from my view as they kissed.

They stood there motionless together for a long moment. Then she settled back onto her heels and ran her hand down his thin body. In the mirror she smiled up with him and then her silver eye caught mine and the smile vanished and I pushed into the room so hard the door hit the wall.

They both yelled something at once and Lilith spun to face me. I grabbed her by the shoulders and threw her into the closet's sliding doors, knocking them down with a clatter of metal and one sharp crack of breaking glass. Lucas was stumbling backwards, raising his hands to protect his face as I swung at him with my right fist. I hit his forearm twice and then his face, knocking him back against the small table next to the bed. I hit him with my left and he took the table down with him to the floor. Lilith yelled something that I couldn't understand and I heard another crack of glass.

I stood over Lucas, fist raised, breathing hard.

Lucas was laughing, trying to cover his face.

"Fuck!" he said.

And then I felt a stab of pain and my stomach clenched into a knot. Every muscle locked up like a spring-loaded trap and I doubled over and liquid rushed up and exploded from my mouth. White liquid gushed out of me. I vomited white liquid down on Lucas and his laughing stopped. His breath caught. And then he began to scream.

He writhed on the floor, drenched in what looked like white paint, screaming. Little red dots began to appear in the white, and then blood poured out of him, all at once, from all over his body. His skin was gone. His eyelids and lips were gone. The white liquid pour down into his naked teeth and his screams turned to gurgles. His teeth were gone. His eyes were gone. His body thrashed on the floor and it was getting smaller and smaller. The gurgling cut off in a ragged, high-pitched shriek and suddenly the only sound was stunted limbs thrashing on the carpet and the wet crackling of ligaments and bones coming apart. His arms and legs were gone. He was a chunk of a torso and a knob of a head, curling up on itself like a dying worm. And then there was nothing left but liquid.

There was a moment of silence and then Lilith screamed and then the white liquid separated itself from the red and began to coalesce and suck itself inward into a pool. The liquid surged towards me over the floor, over my shoes, up my pant legs and under my shirt, and forced itself back into my mouth, my nose, my tear ducts and my pores all at once, the pressure in my head building and building and then suddenly it was over.

I stood there clutching my face. The pain was gone. Lucas was gone. Where he had been, there was nothing but blood. Blood had sprayed up onto the walls and the bed sheets. The carpet so dark red it was almost black. I heard a choked sob behind me and I turned. Lilith was standing there with her hands over her mouth. Her eyes were wild and vacant, staring at nothing.

I tried to speak. My lungs were trying to breathe faster than they could. "I don't—" I said and Lilith screamed in pain and rage.

I threw up my arms as a reflex as she came at me. She sank her teeth into my forearm and shook her head violently like a dog, ripping out a chunk of my flesh. I saw it happen, I screamed, but it happened too fast for me to feel it. Then I was back against the wall and the sharp points of her teeth were sinking into my neck and pain exploded finally in my arm.

I tried to say something but I couldn't breathe. Her jaw was tightening and I could feel her teeth digging in to my throat. I could feel each individual point.

And then she let me go and fell onto the bed, sobbing. I stared down at my arm. It was pouring blood. A large piece was missing. I stumbled into the bathroom and ripped up a wad of paper towel and pressed it against the wound as hard as I could.

"You killed him!" she screamed from the bedroom.

I stood in front of the sink and watched the paper towel turn red.

***

"Jesus, dude," said Tom.

We were standing in the bedroom door, a grown man and a pre-adolescent boy looking in on a blood-drenched room. It wasn't red anymore, everything was stained rusty brown. The air smelled metallic.

"You really shouldn't have done that, man," said Tom.

"Are you fucking kidding me?" I said. "I didn't mean to do it. I still don't even know what happened."

"Well, I do," said Tom. "That Milk shit is fucking dangerous. How do you think they turned me into a kid, man? Waving a fucking magic wand? They put me into the Milk, the same shit you've been putting into your body for months, and the Milk fucking dissolved me, dissolved my whole body and reformed me as a little kid. This is not stuff you should be fucking around with."

"So this stuff has just been gathering in my body? What is it, a weapon? I just don't understand," I said. "I wasn't going to kill him." My hands were still shaking. There was a deep, pulsing ache in my arm. The bleeding was finally under control. I'd stuffed the wound with paper towel and wrapped it tightly in duct tape.

"But you were angry right?"

"Yeah," I said. "I was angry. It was stupid, I was just angry and jealous. I wasn't thinking straight."

"Well, look," said Tom. "I don't know what happened, but I do know that the guy who was fucking your girlfriend is now missing and your apartment is absolutely drenched in his blood. Where is that chick anyway?"

"I don't know," I said.

"Fuck, do you think she went to the cops? Does she know about cops and all that?" Tom was pacing in a tight circle, staring down at his small tennis shoes. "Ok, here's what we're going to do: we're going to clean this shit up as fast as we can and we're going to do it well. We need equipment and cleaning supplies, of course. We'll clean the carpet so well luminol won't even work on it, we'll lift it up and clean the cement underneath. It's going to take a while, we need to get started. But, seriously, who better for the job than us, right?"

"Any other professional crime-scene cleaners would be better than us," I said. "Anyone who didn't spend every day getting high and half-assing every job."

"The point is," said Tom. "This isn't even a hard job. It's just blood. There aren't even any chunks for us to get rid of. It's easy, we just need the right equipment. And once we get this cleaned up, the cops won't have shit on you. There's no body. No evidence. No story that chick can tell them will make any sense at all because, seriously, this shit doesn't make any sense at all. Do you still have keys to the office? It would be easier to just steal everything from work."

I opened my mouth to speak and the front door opened behind us. My insides turned to ice.

"Fuck!" said Tom, spinning around.

I turned. Lilith was standing in the doorway. Her hair was a mess and her eyes were red and swollen from crying. Her shirt was splattered with my blood. Her arms were wrapped tightly around her waist.

"Lilith," I said, "I don't know what happened. Please..."

"I know," she said. Her face was calm but I could see hatred in her eyes. "I know you didn't... control what happened. You didn't mean to kill. You were only trying to hurt him. And me."

"I'm sorry, Lilith," my voice shook as I spoke.

"Be quiet," she said. "I know what we need to do now. We will leave. Now. We will never come back here. We will go down below and meet with the Olm and we will become children, like your friend. And we will go into the sky with the others. I cannot be here. And I cannot look at your face. I cannot stand to look at you."

A new sort of panic was growing in me. I opened my mouth to speak.

"Be quiet!" she said. "I could have torn your throat open. I felt your life's pulse under my teeth. You do not deserve to live as you are now, after what you have done. But I'm giving you a chance to start again."

I looked back and forth between her and Tom. Tom stood frozen, like a rabbit.

"You will do this thing," she said.

My head was spinning. I put my hand against the door frame.

"You'll come with me?" I said. "Up into the sky?"

Her jaw tightened. "Yes," she said.

The three of us left the apartment, the blood-stained room, the fallen closet doors with the broken mirror, the toppled side-table, the broken dirty plate, the fallen glass pipe and spilled weed, the crumpled, bloodied paper towels all over the bath room floor, the empty bottles of beer and vodka in the living room and the jug of Milk on the counter. We never came back.

***

Lilith stayed a few yards ahead of us in the tunnel. She didn't speak or look back.

"I told you she was trouble," said Tom in a low voice.

"You told me she was a lizard," I said. "And I don't really want to have this conversation right now."

"Well, lizard or not, she was threatening to rip your fucking throat out with her teeth back there," said Tom. "Or was I confused?"

"I killed Lucas," I said. "I murdered him."

"No, you vomited some weird liquid onto him that dissolved him. That's not any form of murder I've ever heard of. Got to be manslaughter at most, right? It's not like you were planning on dissolving him with vomit, were you?" he said. "It's just really bad luck for you, is what it is."

"Bad luck?"

"Well yeah," he said. "You killed this guy, accidentally killed this guy, right when your lady friend there was all crushing on him and shit. So now, not only will she hate you forever, but she'll also always remember that douche as some perfect guy she was madly in love with. It's like frozen in her mind, that he's some great guy, because he didn't live long enough for her to find out what a douche he actually was."

"Shut up, Tom."

"I'm just saying, she would've gotten tired of him, too, if—"

"Shut the fuck up, Tom."

We all rode the elevator down together. No one spoke and Lilith kept her eyes straight ahead.

***

Only when we stepped out onto the crowded below-ground streets did she look at me, clearly confused.

"I know," I said.

"All these people…" she said.

"It was like this yesterday too," I said. Was it yesterday? Or two days ago? I couldn't remember. "I don't understand it either."

We pushed our way through the crowd. Street vendors showed off their products, talking quickly and loudly in languages I didn't recognize. I saw Lilith wave a few of them off with a shake of her head and a few words in the same language. Tom stuck close to me. The crowd towered over him. A group of children with painted faces watched him pass, then turned to whisper excitedly to each other.

"I refuse to hold your fucking hand," Tom had to speak loudly to be heard above the din, "but for the love of god, don't lose me in this crowd, man!"

Lilith was back out in front of us again, though she occasionally glanced back to make sure we were still behind her. I couldn't remember how to get to the Olm's place without her, I had always followed her there before. I hadn't bothered to pay attention.

We turned off onto a slightly less crowded side street and at last I recognized the place. The Olm's room was below street level, down some cement stairs. While most of the buildings now had signs and customers, the stairs leading down to the Olm's room remained dark and unlabeled. The business above it looked like a beauty salon. A woman inside the front window was rubbing a child's face with thick white paint, holding a tube in her mouth and breathing out clouds of smoke as she worked.

Tom tripped behind me on the way down the stairs and fell against my back.

"Fuck!" he said. "I can't see shit."

Lilith shot an annoyed glance over her shoulder. When she made eye contact with me she flinched and quickly looked away.

She reached the door at the bottom of the stairs and put her hand on the knob and paused for a moment. It was a blank wooden door, painted white, as it had always been. There were no windows. She tested the knob. It turned. She pushed the door open and I heard the familiar jingling bell.

"Well, well," said a voice from inside. "I love it when old friends come to visit."

***

The Olm sat at his table under his lamp in the dark room, wet pink fingers folded in front of him on the table.

"Please," he said, "have a seat." His tongue flicked out and tasted the air. "Welcome back, Tom, my boy. The procedure went as advertised, yes?"

"Yeah," Tom murmured. "As advertised."

There were three seats in front of the table. We each took one.

"And Lilith, sweetness," said the Olm. "Always a pleasure." His tongue flicked out again. "Sweet indeed. You always are. And of course," he turned his eyeless snout to me. "Jordan. Yes. Long time, no see, am I right? Jordan? Though I must say I was a little hurt when I found out." He reached a hand into his trench coat.

"Found out?" I said. "Found out what?"

"That you, my dear friend, were down here in my town," said the Olm. His hand came out from his trench coat, holding a small glass vial between two fingers. My vial, half full of Milk. "And you didn't pay me a visit. Didn't even say hello."

He held the vial up to the light. Lilith and Tom looked at it, then at me.

"Is there a problem?" I said.

The Olm chuckled. "Well, like I said, my feelings were a little hurt. But I got over it. I'm not even mad about you selling in my territory. Or trading goods for services, as the case may be. I am, however, a little upset about the dead prostitute."

He set the vial down on the table and refolded his

hands in front of him. My heart was racing.

"Dead? What do you mean?"

He shrugged, turning his palms up in the air.

"You killed her, didn't you," I said. "You pathetic, disgusting, evil piece of shit."

The Olm laughed. "Oh, heaven's no! What do you take me for, my boy? More than anything, I am a business man. And killing an extremely lucrative source of income, that is not good business. Of course I didn't kill her, you idiot," the Olm leaned in over the table. "You killed her. This," he shook the vial of Milk in my face, "this is what killed her."

I stared at him, pushed back as far as I could in my seat. "I don't understand," my voice came out as a croak. "I…"

"Did you really think that you could just go up to the lake, gather up some raw Milk, and just start selling it? Did you really think it was that simple?"

"But I filtered it—"

The Olm threw back his head and laughed. "Filtered it! Oh! My god, Jordan, you really are that stupid aren't you? Filtered it! The Milk isn't just some 'dirty liquid' that needs to be purified. This Milk is alive, don't you see? The Milk needs to be told what to do! The Milk that I sell is carefully programmed. It does one thing and one thing only and it does it very well: it gets you high. And then it filters itself out of your bloodstream and leaves through your kidneys and that's that. The raw Milk will get you high, sure, if that's what you're expecting it to do. But then it stays around and does other things. Without explicit instruction, the Milk in your body takes random, undirected input from your brain chemistry, your unconscious, god only knows what else, and based on that preposterous mishmash of data, it 'decides' what to do. You can understand why this is dangerous, yes? Surely!"

The Olm sat back in his chair, licking at his own head and working his little fetus hands in agitation before crossing his arms over his chest. The half-empty vial sat on the table between us. The overhead lamp reflected off the glass in one small bright point, hurting my eyes.

"How did she die?" I said.

The Olm sighed. "She had just finished with a client," he said. "He told me, she just stopped and looked up at the ceiling, like something grabbed her attention, and then Milk and blood, lots of blood, gushed out of her eye sockets and she keeled over dead. Her skull was completely empty. I examined the body myself. It liquefied her brain in an instant, poor girl. At least it was quick."

I remembered her on top of me, smiling down at me. But the smile never touched her dark blue eyes. Every inch of her was covered in freckles. "I don't…" I said, but I couldn't finish the thought. We didn't have sex for the whole hour, because I wasn't up to it. But I paid for the hour. I was happy just having my arms around something warm and soft. She was just watching the clock.

"So!" the Olm said abruptly. "Now that we've covered that little piece of business… whatever did you come here for? Hmm? To what do I owe the pleasure?"

I couldn't answer. Lilith was staring down at her

lap.

"We're here because he wants the procedure," said Tom. "He wants to turn into a child like me, go up the New Equipment, that whole thing."

I think the Olm smiled then, but it's hard to say what a smile would look like on that pink, salamander head. "Good answer," he said. "Best possible answer. Dare I say, the only acceptable answer for you, Jordan. But you Lilith? You too?"

Lilith nodded stiffly. "Yes," she said.

The Olm reached into the other side of his overcoat and brought out two black pills. "Well then," he said. "No need to dilly-dally. The procedure is quite simple. You will swallow this pill. You will take my elevator, it will take you to the shore of the Milk. Submerge yourself completely. The pill has the instructions contained within it, it will analyze your DNA and tell the Milk what to do. And then you will wake up a child. A fresh start, a clean slate! Perfect."

Lilith held out her palm and I did the same. The Olm carefully dropped a pill in each hand.

"Care to show them the way, Tom?" he said. "Do you still remember?"

Tom nodded and pushed his chair back from the table. "Yeah, the elevator's just back here. It's real simple."

The Olm gestured the way. We stood up and followed him out of the pool of lamplight into the darkness. A couple yards away from the table, I turned back briefly. The Olm was still sitting there. He was putting the vial back into his trench coat.

We got on the elevator.

***

The elevator took us up into massive cave with a massive pool of Milk, different than the one I was familiar with. The shoreline stretched off into the darkness to the left and right, dotted by the occasional electric lamp. The Milk stretched off into the darkness ahead. I looked down at the little black pill and the significance of what I was doing finally hit me. My heart raced. My breaths were getting faster and shallower and I felt hot and cold at the same time. This was actually going to happen.

I turned to Lilith and she made eye contact for the first time in hours. She must have seen the panic in my eyes. "You must do this," she said, "or I will never forgive you."

She turned away and began to walk down the shore. "Where are you going?" I said. "Wait."

"I don't want to do this near you," she said.

"But you'll come back when it's over, right?"

"Yes."

"It'll be over in just a few minutes," I said, "and then you'll come back as a little girl. And I'll be a little boy. In just a few minutes."

She was getting smaller and smaller, following the lamps down the shore.

"Promise me I'll see you again," I called after her.

"I promise," she called back.

I watched her disappear in the distance.

I never saw her again.

***

"It's really not that bad," said Tom, looking down at his shoes. "Just take the pill and get in the Milk."

I had been standing there, motionless, staring at the pill for some time now.

"Seriously, if I could do it than you can do it," he said. "It's like starting over fresh, like a reset button."

I didn't do anything. The only sound was Milk gently sloshing on the shore.

"Come on, man," he said. "I already did it and I'm super ready to get up that New Equipment, away from all this bullshit. It's the best thing. Your apartment up there is covered with a dead guy's blood, for Christ's sake. And who knows how long until the lizards start attacking. Even that crazy lady friend you care about so much wants you to do it. Just fucking do it already."

I tossed the pill in my mouth almost without thinking, before I could hesitate any longer. It dissolved instantly on my tongue into a bitter, metallic taste that made me gag.

"There you go!" said Tom. "Now go for a swim."

I waded out into the Milk. My shoes filled with liquid. I was expecting it to be cold, but it was lukewarm, basically the same temperature as my body. I forced my way out further, my pants filling up with liquid and slowing me down as I went, then fell forward and plunged headlong into the pool like a swimmer. Milk rushed into my nose and ears and the familiar acrid taste exploded into my head. There was a moment of muffled calm, floating face down under the surface of the Milk. And then my skin began to tingle.

The tingling started at once, all over my body. And then it grew and turned into an itch, mild at first but intensifying, becoming maddening, like a million tiny insects crawling all over me and then the itch began to burn, building and building into an inferno, like flames, like acid, like my whole body was raw and covered in salt and when I opened my mouth to scream the milk rushed in and the pain hit my gums and tongue and poured down my throat and then I was burning inside and out all at once and I realized I was melting.

And suddenly the pain dropped away and I felt very light.

This is shock, I thought. *I'm going into shock.*

Everything was falling away.

And at that moment I realized that I was dying and I realized I wasn't coming back. The Milk might make a new thing out of my body, a child that looked like me as a child, but it would not be me. It would be something else. This was death, absolute and complete.

And as I realized this, everything just went away, like I was falling asleep and all my thoughts stopped and I was nothing.

And that's the last thing I remember.

Part 3

"Ok, let me explain what's going to happen real quick," said the woman in the tuxedo, scooping vanilla ice cream into a glass dish.

Samantha nodded, trying to look attentive despite the hangover. She couldn't tell if the smell inside the kitchen was making her hungry or sick. The Milk didn't seem to be helping either, it just gave everything a sharp, brittle quality like crumpling tin foil.

"I'm going to bring the Reverend his sundae," said the woman in the tuxedo. "You're going to come with me. Then he's going to show off some stuff he can do, levitate or something."

"Levitate?" said Samantha.

"He'll probably complain that I made the sundae wrong somehow," said the woman in the tuxedo. "And then you two will retire to his bedchambers to do… whatever it is he does with his female callers." She looked Samantha up and down, adding a couple squirts of hot fudge to the ice cream. "You don't really look like a prostitute," she said. "He'll like that. Though the hair color is a bit much."

Samantha reached up and touched her short, metallic gold hair. Her mouth opened and closed once. "I… I'm not a prostitute," she said.

The woman gave her a tight lipped smile. "That's the spirit."

"And you're some kind of… female butler?" said Samantha.

"Something like that," said the woman. "Now, I realize you've never heard of him, but the Reverend considers himself to be a very important individual, so it's best to treat him that way." She sprinkled peanuts on the sundae, stuck a spoon into the ice cream and gestured for Samantha to follow her, walking backwards through the kitchen's swinging doors into a dimly lit hallway with red carpets and wooden paneling on the walls. "Also, in case no one has told you yet, I should probably mention that he has the body of a child."

"The body of a child?" said Samantha. "Like…"

"He appears to be twelve years old," said the woman. "But I think he might actually be an adult.

Mentally, I mean. I'm not really clear on that."

"Ok…" said Samantha.

"So try not to let it… hinder you," said the woman, "in performing your services."

"I told you, I'm not a prostitute," said Samantha.

"Of course you aren't," said the woman.

"And besides, I was told there would be no sex involved."

"Of course you were," said the woman. They arrived at an intricately-carved wooden door that looked like something that someone who had never been in a mansion would expect a mansion to have. "Here we are. Try not to speak unless spoken to. And don't let his appearance fool you, he can kill you instantly with his mind." She knocked briskly on the door. Samantha stood behind her with her hands in her pockets, rocking back and forth on her heels. After a moment, another woman in a tuxedo opened the door and ushered them inside.

In the middle of the room there was a large recliner facing a wall covered in TV screens. Each screen showed a different angle of the inside of some very complex playground equipment.

"I'm telling you," a child's voice was saying, "those muppets are the only thing keeping me from killing myself out of boredom. Seriously, this thing has been boring as shit so far." There was a pause. "Well, tell him that I'm holding up my part of the deal and all I ask is a little goddamn entertainment every once and a while. I want to be entertained, dammit!" Pause. "Ok, ok, hey listen, I got an appointment right now, I got to go. We still on for chasing the ol' dragon later tonight?

Sweet. Yeah dude, gotta catch that H train. Ha ha! Later, bro."

The recliner un-reclined and rotated to face the door. A young child in a business suit was seated in the chair, holding a cellphone. He had a silver dot on his forehead.

"This better be my goddamn sundae already," he said. He held up the cellphone and waved it in the air until a woman in a tuxedo came and took it from him. "Ah good. Took long enough. And who is this nice young lady?"

"Hi, I'm Samantha," said Samantha. The woman shot her a dirty look as she took the ice cream to Reverend Timmy. "The Olm told me to come here."

"She's the new girl you requested, sir," said the woman with the ice cream. "The Olm sent her right over."

Reverend Timmy smiled at Samantha from across the room. "How lovely," he said. He took the bowl of ice cream and looked it over with disapproval. "Peanuts..." he muttered. He set it down on a metal tray attached to the armchair. "So... Samantha," he said. "What do you know about me, the good and honorable Reverend?"

"Oh," said Samantha. "You know... lots of things. Good things. People only ever seem to have good things to say."

"She's from the lower level, sir," said the woman in the tuxedo.

Reverend Timmy glared at her, then went back to smiling at Samantha. "So you know about this?" he said, touching the silver dot on his forehead. "The 'Will to Power Converter'?"

"Sure," said Samantha. "I know... a little about it, sure."

"It's very simple, really," said Reverend Timmy. "It's a very powerful, very ancient device that converts my Will," he held up one hand and looked at it, "into Power." He held up the other hand and looked at it, then folded both on his lap and looked back up at Samantha. "For example. This sundae here. It has peanuts on it. I do not like peanuts. So..." There was a low buzzing sound that made Samantha's teeth itch and the peanuts removed themselves from the ice cream and settled on the tray next to the bowl. "And... whatshername here is the one who put the peanuts on it. And I'm not happy about that. So..." There was a low buzzing sound and the woman in the tuxedo went limp and collapsed to the floor. Samantha stopped rocking back and forth on her heels. The woman convulsed on the carpet a few times and was still. Samantha was beginning to regret borrowing money from the Olm. Reverend Timmy continued to smile at her.

"Don't worry," he said. "She's just unconscious. I'm not really that mad, I'm just making a demonstration, you know?" Two other women in tuxedos hurried over, pulled the unconscious woman up from the ground by her arms and dragged her out of the room. Samantha watched them go. The unconscious woman had begun to bleed from the nose.

"Now then," said Reverend Timmy. He made a gesture and the rest of his servants began to file out of the room. Samantha stood very still with her hands in her pockets and wished she were sober. "You know what I am capable of, and that's good." He began to pick up the peanuts from his tray and put them back on his ice cream. "Except you don't really know what I'm capable of, because I am capable of literally anything. Literally. But showing you all that would take all afternoon." He spooned a couple of bites of the sundae into his mouth. "Want to see me levitate?"

Samantha stared at him. "Sure," she said.

He laughed. "Well, maybe later."

***

Later, Samantha found herself standing at the foot of the good and honorable Reverend Timmy's large, satin sheeted bed. The Reverend was naked.

"Do as I say," Timmy said. "Or I will kill you. Hit me!"

Samantha stared down at him. She found she couldn't move.

"Do it!" he yelled. "Hit me with the belt!"

"I don't…" she said. "This is really fucked up."

"Of course it's fucked up, that's why it's so hot! Hit me or I will fucking—"

Samantha hit him with the belt.

"Harder, you bitch! Didn't it make you mad, the way I hurt that woman for no reason?"

She hit him again.

"Harder! For no fucking reason! I gave her a fucking seizure or something! Jesus, I'm a piece of shit! Tell me I'm shit!"

She hit him again. "You're a piece of shit," she said.

"Again! More!"

"Shut up, you pathetic fuck! Don't tell me what to say!"

"Yes!"

"You worthless shit. You spoiled little brat!"

"Yes! Harder!"

"I told you to shut up! Asshole! Pathetic child!"

"Ow! Yes!"

"Does that hurt? Does it?"

"Oh god…"

"Worthless… stupid… child…"

"Tell me no one will ever love me."

"I already told you to shut up, so…"

"Ow!"

"Shut your fucking mouth!"

***

A different female butler led Samantha back to the elevator. Neither of them spoke. On the long elevator ride down, Samantha decided that she really needed a drink. There was a ding as the elevator reached the ground floor. Samantha gave the butler woman a nod and tight-lipped smile and stepped out into the marble lobby of the elevator building. She crossed the lobby and exited the building, a tremendous tower of glass and metal that stretched up into the sky, emblazoned with the name "Timmy" in gold letters above the automatic sliding doors.

Out on the street, the feeling of claustrophobia began to lessen the further she got from the tower. She walked downtown to a bar called the White Jimba and ordered two shots of tequila and a beer. She downed the shots back to back, and took a swig of beer.

The room was dark. The only light was provided by the glowing white surfaces of the tables and the bar itself and flat white lights behind the shelves of liquor bottles. The white light pulsed in time to the music in the background, something electronic that thumped and buzzed. Samantha began to nod her head slightly to the beat. The warm glow of tequila was spreading in her stomach like a magical potion of healing. She was already feeling better. She had begun feeling better the instant alcohol touched her lips.

She rotated her stool around backwards and surveyed the room, elbows propped on the bar behind her. Fresh out of debt. And with a little extra money from the good Reverend himself. Really not that bad a deal, all things considered. The bar was moderately busy this evening, bustling with life but not crowded.

She remembered getting lost in a frenzy earlier, hitting Timmy with the belt over and over. And then his breath caught mid-scream and he sort of tensed up and shook. She had stopped immediately, terrified. She realized a moment later that he was ejaculating onto the bedspread. Then he fell down on the bed next to his pool of semen and curled up into a fetal position. He lay there and cried for what seemed like an eternity. His back and legs were covered with welts. Samantha had stood there with the belt, trying to look at everything in the room except the crying little boy. There's a table, there's a lamp...

Samantha rotated herself back around to face the bar and ordered another shot.

After a few more minutes and another beer, she was beginning to feel bouncy and cheerful. A woman came up to the bar next to her and ordered herself some mixed drink Samantha had never heard of. The woman looked to be about the same age as Samantha, maybe a few years older. She was very pale, essentially colorless in the cold white light of the glowing bar. Samantha shot her a friendly smile. The woman smiled back apprehensively.

"You meeting people here?" said Samantha.

"I'm sorry?" said the woman, looking even more apprehensive.

"I was just wondering if you have friends coming, or if you're drinking alone. The way the cool people do, you know?" Samantha pointed at herself and giggled. She was beginning to feel a little apprehensive herself. "I'm sorry, I'm kind of drunk."

The other woman laughed and sat down on the barstool next to her. "That's ok," she said. "I will be drunk soon enough. And no, I am not meeting friends."

"My name's Samantha," said Samantha. "And I've had a really weird day. How about you?"

The woman smiled. Her teeth were pointed. "My day hasn't been so weird, Samantha," she said. "Not so good though either. Like most days recently. My name is Lilith."

"Well, let me buy you a shot, Lilith," said Samantha. "You have some catching up to do."

***

Samantha tried to get up from her stool and nearly fell over. Lilith caught her by the arm, laughing.

"Be more careful!" she said.

"I am trying to do that," said Samantha.

"Try more!" said Lilith.

"I'm trying to try more!" said Samantha. "You know, I think I'm just going to sit back down for a second right here. Yes. Sitting is good. I have decided that I don't really have to pee that badly after all."

Lilith was still laughing. "Come on, I'll help you."

"No, no, I'm ok. I'm good. Let's get another drink. You want another drink?" Samantha swung around and leaned back against the bar and began to rummage through her pockets. They were all empty. "Ah, goddamn it," she said.

"I'll buy these ones, it's ok," said Lilith. "What do you want to drink?"

"Something with alcohol in it," said Samantha.

Lilith flagged down the bartender and ordered two Long Island iced teas.

"How do you know all these fancy drink names?" said Samantha, verifying for the third time that her beer bottle was empty.

"They have lots of bars up on the surface," said Lilith. "For a long time, they've had them. They didn't used to have any bars like this down here. Things have changed so much. There didn't used to be any of this."

"What'd you mean? I always come here," said Samantha. "What's the surface?"

"This wasn't even here!" said Lilith. She leaned in and put her arm on Samantha's shoulder. "How long have you been in this city?"

"My whole life," said Samantha. "This bar's always been here."

Lilith didn't say anything. Samantha turned to look

at her. Lilith had a strange expression that Samantha couldn't interpret. She couldn't make her eyes focus properly.

"Everyone keeps saying this," said Lilith. "No one remembers how it was before."

"How what was?"

Lilith shook her head, "Forget it, forget it," she said. She slid Samantha her drink and poked her playfully in the arm. "You. I like your hair."

Samantha gasped and leaned backwards, almost falling over again. "Aww!" she said.

"It's shiny," said Lilith.

"It is shiny!" said Samantha. "You're nice. You're a nice person."

***

Samantha found herself stumbling down a street, her arm around Lilith's shoulder. The ground seemed to be moving violently in all directions.

Lilith was saying something to her.

"What?" said Samantha.

"Where do you live? I'll take you to your home."

"Wherever," said Samantha. "I'm ok, really. I can find my way."

Lilith laughed. "You can't even stand up without me holding you, where do you live?"

"Anywhere," said Samantha. "Really, I'm ok."

"Don't you live somewhere?"

"I am living somewhere. I'm living. And I'm somewhere? Right? Seriously, I'm fine." Samantha tried to push herself away from Lilith. Lilith caught her arm and there was a blur of street lights and then

Samantha felt her head hit the ground but it didn't hurt at all.

Lilith was on top of her, laughing, trying to stand up. Samantha was staring up at a streetlight that had become three street lights.

"Come on," Lilith was tugging on her hand. "Stand up. Can you stand up?"

"No," said Samantha. "I cannot... do that."

"Come on, I can't lift you by myself."

"I don't wanna."

"You have to try to do it, Samantha. Here, I'll put your arm around my neck. Now, when I count to three..."

***

"Where are we?" said Samantha. They were climbing a metal stairway.

"My home. Here, I want you to sit down right here while I unlock the door. Sit, I don't want you to stand next to the edge."

Samantha sat down on the cement. Her back was resting against a metal railing.

There was a jingling sound as Lilith tried to take her keys out of her pocket.

"I didn't need keys before either," she muttered. She pulled the keys out and something small and hard fell out of her pocket and hit the cement next to Samantha.

"You dropped something," Samantha said. She leaned over very slowly to pick it up.

"This door," said Lilith. "So irritating..."

"Looks like a little black pill," said Samantha, holding it up in front of her.

"What?" said Lilith.

"Is it something fun? Were you hiding something fun, Lilith?"

Lilith snatched the pill from between her fingers.

"Ow!" said Samantha.

"Not fun," said Lilith. "It's not drugs like you think. I'm sorry I hurt your fingers. It's dangerous."

"What is it?" said Samantha. She was struggling to keep her eyes open.

Lilith dropped the pill and stepped on it. It crunched. She kicked at the powder and crumbs a few times, off the edge of the balcony. "Nothing," she said.

Samantha heard the jingling of keys, then the click of a lock. She couldn't keep her eyes open anymore.

"Come on, Samantha," someone was tugging on her arm again. "Get up."

***

"And then I woke up in the cave, washed up on the shore," said Jordan, "and you helped me up and we left."

Tom nodded, but didn't say anything. This was not the first time they had discussed this.

They were sharing a seat on an old school bus. They looked out the window and watched the scenery go past.

Then Jordan said: "I don't really like being a child."

"It isn't that bad," said Tom, looking down at his swinging feet.

"I don't like being small like this. My arms and legs are short, it takes forever to get anywhere. My voice is all high. I feel like I have a hard time concentrating."

"Jesus Christ, dude," said Tom. "All adults do is

bitch about wanting to be kids again. And then when you give them the chance to actually do it, what do they do? They bitch about that too."

"Come on," said Jordan, "you can't tell me you haven't had some second thoughts about this whole thing."

"Nope," said Tom. "No point to it."

Jordan felt a sudden tightness in his throat and a stinging in his eyes. He realized he was suddenly on the verge of tears and he wasn't sure why.

"Are we even the same people anymore?" he said.

Tom propped his elbow up on the metal edge of the window, glaring at the seat in front of him. "What do you mean? I get what you're saying about the short attention span and everything. And I feel antsy, like it's hard to sit still. I get that. But I'm still me. I still remember my whole life from before. I still act like me, don't I? You still act like you."

Jordan took some deep, slow breaths. "All I know is my whole body dissolved. I felt everything dissolve, the skin, the muscle, the bone—"

"Jesus Christ, would you shut up about that part already?"

"You felt it all too, didn't you?"

"Yeah, man. I fucking felt it. I was awake and conscious right up to the very end and I don't like thinking about it. Don't make me think about that shit," said Tom. "It's done, it's over with."

"And you didn't warn me," said Jordan.

They sat in silence for a moment. Other children chattered around them. They bus shuddered and rattled over every small bump in the road.

"You know, caterpillars dissolve completely in their cocoon," said Tom. "They don't just grow wings, they turn into a soup and completely reform, basically like we did in the Milk."

"So is the butterfly really the same as the caterpillar?"

"Well," said Tom. "I mean... you can't really... It's just an insect, it doesn't have hopes and dreams and shit. I still have all the same hopes and dreams I had before, so I'm still me. It's not the same as with an insect. It was a stupid comparison, I guess."

They were quiet again.

"Did you know that every seven years, every single atom in your body gets replaced?" said Tom. "When you turned twenty-one, not a single particle in your body was left over from when you were fourteen. And the fourteen-year-old version of you didn't have a single atom left from the seven-year-old version. You see how that works? But you were still the same person despite that, right?"

"Yeah, I guess so," said Jordan. He remembered dissolving, and he was pretty sure he remembered what it felt like to die, but he didn't say anything else about it.

As the bus rounded the curve of the mountain, the New Equipment came into view, a tremendous column silhouetted black against the sky and stretching up out of sight into the clouds.

"Fuck, dude," said Tom, pressing his face up against the bus window. "Look at this thing, man! I can't get over it."

Tom had taken Jordan to meet with Reverend

Timmy shortly after the transformation. Reverend Timmy was a child of the same general age as Tom and Jordan and the rest of the group. He always wore suits and had a shiny silver dot on his forehead between his eyes, a circle about a centimeter across. No one ever said anything about the dot, but Jordan assumed it held some religious significance.

They were supposed to do a month of proselytizing before they would be allowed to take the actual trip to the New Equipment, but they ended up just stuffing envelopes and recruiting online. The door-to-door program had been shut down. Once the "children's cult" got all over the news, people started calling the cops.

Tom had been allowed to see the New Equipment once before. All new inductees were taken on a bus to view the Equipment from a distance, to see the massive structure in person. It was much easier to convince adults to undergo the transformation process after they had witnessed it for themselves, the giant tower to the sky.

"Beautiful, isn't it?" the kid in the seat in front of them said. Jordan recognized him. His name was Isaiah. He had seen the kid at the pre-ascension party the night before. Tom and Jordan and most of the kids spent the night drinking and smoking weed, enjoying the low tolerances of their undersized bodies, but Isaiah had made a point of abstaining, sitting in the corner reading the literature, giving the rest of the kids the occasional smug, judgmental glance.

"It's a hell of a thing alright," said Jordan.

"It's glorious!" said Isaiah. "Even more sublime

than I remembered."

"It's really fucking big," said Tom.

Isaiah gave them a tight-lipped smile around the edge of the seat. "It has to be," he said, "to reach all the way to heaven."

Jordan looked out the window past Tom's head.

The school bus wound its way down the mountain and the equipment grew and grew. It began to take on detail. The roughly cylindrical shape was ragged with random outcroppings and parapets. As they traveled towards it, it seemed to flatten out in front of them, losing its discernible curve and becoming a wall, a tangled web of brightly colored ladders and slides, catwalks and scaffolding, towers of bricks, cement and glass, an impossibly complex convolution of metal and plastic like the mutated offspring of every skyscraper and playground in the world multiplied a million times and sprouting organically from the desert floor. It stretched up into the sky, tapering off into a vanishing point above them, a glorious and deranged orgy of architecture like nothing else Jordan had ever seen. Surely like nothing else on this world or the even the world below it.

Finally the bus came to stop about a hundred yards out and the children began to file out, gazing upwards in awe and reverence.

Jordan paused by the bus driver, stepping out of the way to let others past.

"Excuse me," he said. "I was just wondering if you'd seen someone I know. Maybe on some of your other trips out here. A little girl."

The bus driver was a large, bald man. He turned

to look at Jordan.

"Short blond hair, silver eyes. Like a cat's eyes. The pupils are vertical, like this," he made an up-and-down motion with his finger. "She has pointy teeth. If you saw her teeth."

The bus driver stared at him with blank eyes.

"Real pale," said Jordan.

"Come on." Tom was tugging on his sleeve.

The bus driver didn't say anything. Tom and Jordan got off the bus. The bus driver watched them go. When the last child was off the bus, he closed the door, made a large u-turn in the desert sand and drove off back the way he came.

***

The children were led into the New Equipment single file through a metal turnstile. Inside, it was a jungle gym in the true sense of the word "jungle." It was impossible to see more than a few yards in any direction through the dense, colorful metal and plastic foliage. Once through the turnstile, the children split up into small groups and wandered off in different directions. As Reverend Timmy had explained in the pre-bus-ride pep-talk, there would be no guides or signs pointing the way to the top in the New Equipment. Each child must find his own way. Jordan assumed the goal was to try to head in a generally upward direction.

Some children began climbing immediately. Jordan and Tom headed off down a shaded rubber pathway by themselves. As they moved deeper into the Equipment, the excited sounds of children receded behind them.

"This shit goes on for miles," said Tom. "It's crazy! How are we supposed to know when to start climbing? What if there's only one way to the top? How would we ever find it?"

Jordan shrugged.

As they got further and further from the entrance the path grew darker. Though it was noon on a cloudless summer day, the sunlight had trouble penetrating the dense tangle of ladders, monkey bars, bridges, dangling ropes and plastic tunnels. Electric lamps began to appear along the edge of the pathway, seemingly at random, dangling from wires and attached to poles protruding out at odd angles from all sides.

The path split into two and they arbitrarily chose left. It split again and they went right. Finally, the path reached a dead end at tangle of curved ladders, arching up and around each other into the maze above.

"Well, I guess this is as good a place as any to start climbing," said Tom, setting his backpack on the ground and placing his hands on his hips in an assertive Superman pose. "Pick a ladder."

"What difference does it make?" said Jordan. "We have no idea where we're going."

"Just pick one, dammit!"

Jordan sighed and shook his head.

"Eenie meenie minie moe," Tom began.

"Ok, ok, don't start with that shit," said Jordan. "The blue one. Let's go with the blue one."

"After you, boss."

They began to climb.

***

"Look at it this way, man," said Tom, "at least now you have a goal in life."

They stood on a rubberized metal grating. They

had been moving upwards for some time now, at least a couple of hours. It was difficult to judge time without the sun. The light seemed to be entirely artificial at this point. Jordan leaned out over the railing at the edge of the platform looking down into the tangled jungle of the Equipment. There was no sign of other children.

"Admit it," said Tom, "You didn't have any real goals back on the surface. I sure as hell didn't. And now look at us, all we have to do is climb this goddamn ridiculous contraption, whatever this thing is, and get to the top. That's better than nothing, right?"

Jordan took off his backpack and knelt down to rifle through it.

"Sure, it may not be 'heaven' at the top," said Tom. "But there's got to be something, right? Some new and different place. It's got to be interesting, whatever it is. Aren't you at least curious?"

Jordan took a brown paper bag out of his backpack. He rummaged through the crumpled balls of newspaper inside and took out a vial of Milk. He held it up to the light, shook it.

"I can't believe you're still doing that shit, dude," said Tom.

"Why wouldn't I?" said Jordan. He unscrewed the top and sucked some liquid into the dropper.

"Well there you fucking go," said Tom. "Still a fucking addict, I guess you are the same person after all."

"I guess so," said Jordan. He placed one small drop on his tongue. The familiar bitter taste filled his mouth. The taste reminded him of Lilith. He remembered kneeling at her feet, his hands on her waist looking up at her. She'd said: "Stick out your tongue."

He screwed the top back on the bottle and put it back in the bag. He put the bag back into the backpack.

"It's the safe stuff anyway," said Jordan. "I got it from the Olm. It's fine."

Tom was looking at him. Jordan could see his image begin to sharpen, tiny lines on Tom's little boy face coming into focus, peach fuzz on his cheeks, every slightly out of place hair catching the light. His expression radiated concern and bemusement.

Jordan laughed. "You look ridiculous," he said. "I never bothered trying to imagine you as a little kid before we changed. It's so weird seeing you this young!"

Tom's mouth curved upwards slightly.

"So aren't you at least curious?" said Tom.

"About what?"

"About what's at the top."

"I guess," said Jordan. It was coming on fast now, he could feel it, a lightness in his body.

"Well why are you going through with this whole thing anyway?" said Tom. "What's your motivation here?"

Jordan shrugged. "It's something to do, isn't it?" he said. "It's not like I have anything better to do."

"What are you grinning about?" said Tom.

"The ripples moving through your skin," said Jordan.

Tom shook his head, chuckling. "Jesus, dude."

"We're moving all the time, even when we're standing still. Can you feel it?"

"Man…" Tom slung his backpack up onto his

shoulder, "I should have brought some weed. Maybe I'd be able to understand what the fuck you're talking about. Come on, let's get going. Onwards and upwards and shit. Upwards and onwards."

Jordan put on his backpack and they headed up a twisting stairway of the same metal grating. The metal's rubber coating was intensely blue under the electric light. The steps seemed to go on forever and for a moment Jordan thought he was stuck in some kind of loop, climbing the same two steps over and over again for eternity. But then they were at the top.

"Every moment is eternal," he said to himself, "but then it's over."

He felt the ground underneath him shift and swing sideways and suddenly he was looking down a great distance into a tangle of brightly colored metal and he realized they were on a rope bridge. He struggled to right himself, clinging to the nylon rope handrail. Tom grabbed his backpack and pulled him away from the edge.

"Jesus, dude! Just watch what you're doing, ok?" said Tom. "Don't be that kid who was so high he thought he could fly or whatever the fuck. Don't turn into an anti-drug commercial on me, for Christ's sake."

***

"Being a child is weird," said Tom. They were climbing hand over hand up a knotted rope made of interwoven strands of blue plastic thread.

"Everything is weird," said Jordan. "Look around."

"Ok, fair enough," said Tom. "But what I mean is, it feels weird trying to move this little body around, you know? Like my brain expects my hands to be bigger.

And I expect to be stronger. But then, my body doesn't weigh a whole lot, so moving myself around actually isn't that difficult. But it kind of is? I dunno."

He reached the top of the rope and climbed up on the platform, rotating his body to get a foot up over the edge. He flopped over, rolling sideways onto his backpack, then awkwardly pushed himself up onto his feet and went back to the platform edge. He reached down and grabbed Jordan's outstretched hand, leaning backwards to help pull him up.

"Ugh," said Tom. "Ok that settles it. Moving around is a pain in the ass for sure. The negatives outweigh the positives. Not that many advantages to being a tiny little shit."

"It could be worse," said Jordan. "We could be actual little kids."

"What'd you mean 'actual'?" said Tom. "We're pretty fucking little, man."

They crossed the platform over to short plastic slide.

"What I mean is," said Jordan, turning around to lower himself down the slide, walking carefully backwards and gripping the edge to stay on his feet. "Little kids with the brains of little kids. Kid's don't have great motor skills. They haven't been around long enough to know how to move well. We may be kind of awkward, but we still have all those years of experience moving around and, like, dealing with physics and shit. That stuff stayed in our brains when we made the switch."

Tom slid down the slide, landing on his feet at the bottom and stumbling forward as the backpack weight through him off balance. Jordan dodged to the side to avoid being bowled over.

"Shit!" said Tom. "I guess you're right, but still. Not very graceful over here."

"Well you weren't the most coordinated person in the world before, were you?"

"Fuck you," said Tom, "I was an elegant motherfucker."

"I'm just saying you weren't exactly a trained dancer or whatever," said Jordan.

"You don't know," said Tom. "You don't know my life, bro."

Jordan laughed.

***

"You've got to be fucking kidding me," said Tom.

"What is it?" said Jordan, pulling himself up onto the platform. They were both out of breath from climbing three consecutive ladders to the top of a multi-tiered tower.

"It just ends here," said Tom, "at these monkey bars."

The square platform was surrounded on three sides by a fine wire mesh that stretched up into the Equipment. The side without the mesh opened into nothing, a fifty-foot drop into a tangle of colorful metal rebar below. Dangling just off the edge of the platform about five feet above was a long row of metal bars, essentially a horizontal ladder suspended by cables. It stretched across the chasm to another platform about twelve feet away.

"This is fucked," said Tom.

"No kidding," said Jordan.

They stood in silence for a moment.

"So… what should we do?" said Jordan.

"Goddamn it," said Tom. "What is the point of all this anyway? Why do we have to go through this ridiculous obstacle-course-from-hell to get to the top? Why wouldn't they just build another elevator like all the other fucking elevators between levels? None of this makes sense."

"You're only now realizing this?" said Jordan with a faint smile. He was trying to remember when his last dosage of Milk had been. He was craving another. His head was buzzing.

"Well, I mean," said Tom, "I don't know. Fuck. What do we do, man?"

Jordan shrugged. "I guess we have to go back."

"How long have we been climbing? When was the last branching off point? It's been hours, it would take hours to backtrack and try to find another way up! Fuck, man! And then what if we did find another way up and it just dead-ended too? This is bullshit."

"Or we could climb across."

"Are you kidding me? Did you look off the edge here? It's dangerous as shit!"

"Well, those are pretty much our only two options," said Jordan.

Tom paced back and forth on the platform, cursing and muttering. Jordan stood still, holding onto his backpack straps.

"Ok," said Tom. "Ok, well… It's not really that far across, right? I mean it would be no problem at all if it weren't for that drop. It wouldn't even be like an endurance test, I don't think. We could throw our backpacks across." He paced some more, staring at his feet. "It's really more of a mental thing, I guess. It's about fear. Seriously man, it feels like we're being fucked with here."

Jordan laughed. "You think?"

"I mean, the other platform has ladders going up…" He stopped and looked up at Jordan, eyebrows raised.

"So you think we should climb across, then," said Jordan.

"Well, I don't know, I mean, it's super fucking dangerous, man. What do you think? I don't know. On the one hand it seems easy, but shit, I'm not going to lie, I'm afraid. I'm fucking terrified."

Jordan sighed and dropped his backpack off his shoulders. He walked to the edge and grabbed on to the first bar with both hands and stepped off the edge.

"Jesus dude!" said Tom.

Jordan reached out to the second bar, grabbed on, released the first and swung to the third. The monkey bars swayed minutely back and forth as he moved.

"Be careful!" Tom called after him. "Fuck!"

Jordan was trying very hard not to look down. His heart was pounding. He was almost half-way across already.

"Doing good man!" said Tom. "I'll throw you the backpacks when you—"

Jordan cried out in pain, yanking his hand away from the bar in front of him.

"Fuck! What happened?" said Tom.

"Something sharp," said Jordan. He was only holding on one hand now, his left hand clutching the bar above, his right hand held out in front of him. Blood was pouring from a deep, ragged gash in the palm.

"Oh fuck, oh fuck," said Tom. "Come back! Come back this way!"

Jordan looked around frantically, over his shoulder at Tom, up at the monkey bars, down at the metal bramble fifty feet below. He was getting paler and paler.

"Don't look down!" said Tom. "Come back here, I'll grab your legs! Come on Jordan, please, man, please!"

Jordan twisted around and made a grab for the bar behind him. He cried out in pain and his bloodied hand slipped off the bar. His body twisted wildly as he flailed with his free hand and tried to make another grab and then he lost his grip with his left and he dropped from the bars. Tom's stomach turned to ice. Jordan let out one terrified shout from somewhere below and then there was the wet thud of meat and reverberating metal.

Tom stood, paralyzed.

"Jordan!"

He fell onto his hands and knees at the edge of the platform and looked down. Jordan's body lay tangled in blood-spattered rebar, the limbs bent at odd angles. His head dangled from his neck.

"Jordan!" yelled Tom. "Say something! Say something to me!"

A wave of dizziness hit Tom and he pushed himself back from the edge. He had begun to shake all over.

"Oh my god," he said over and over. "Oh my god, oh my god..."

***

It took Jordan a few minutes to die. At first, he was in great pain, but then shock set in. Dying was going pretty much the same the second time around. It actually did get a little easier the more he did it.

He was looking up through the tangle of colorful metal bars that had broken his bones, his view swaying slightly left and right. Right around the time he stopped breathing, a cloud of tiny white jellyfish had arrived. They drifted about his broken body like snow. They landed on his face and dipped their tendrils in the tears from his eyes and cheeks.

Things were getting quiet and dark again.

He wondered, for the first time, why he couldn't remember anything from his childhood. His original childhood. Who were his parents? He couldn't remember.

Think of something nice, he thought.

And then he died.

Up above, Tom sat crying. A tiny white jelly fish drifted down through the air, floating on the breeze, occasionally pulsating its coin-sized body to push itself closer to the heat of Tom's body. It touched his cheek, brushing the skin just below his eye with the thin wisps of its thread-like tendrils, and he brushed it away with the back of his hand.

***

Tom woke up on the platform sometime later. He didn't remember falling asleep. He had no idea how much time had passed. Everything was the same as it had been. It was quiet.

He crawled over to the edge and looked down and immediately regretted it. He pulled back and fell over onto his side. He lay there for an indeterminate length of time.

Later, he found himself taking things out of Jordan's backpack and putting them into his own. He didn't remember deciding to do that, but he was doing it. It felt better to do something. Along with the energy bars and MREs and bottles of water that had been provided by the cult, he found Jordan's vial of Milk in a paper bag. He put that into his backpack also.

When his backpack was full, so full it was difficult to close the zipper, he took it and headed back down the tower of platforms, back the way they'd come. He left Jordan backpack where it was.

The air was still. The smell of death only got stronger on the way down.

***

"Hey!" Tom called out. He saw movement up ahead through the tangle of metal bars. "Hey you!"

There was no reply, but more movement. He was pretty sure he could make out the shape of another child. He weaved around ladders and slides, trying to head in that direction through the maze.

"Just hold on a second, for Christ's sake," said Tom. "I'm another one of the kids from the bus."

He was getting closer. It was definitely another child.

"What do you want?" said the child. Tom was almost there now.

"I want to know what the fuck is going on, is what I want," said Tom. "I just watched my friend die and I want to know what the fuck is going on. Isaiah? Is that you?"

Tom squeezed through a hexagonal hole and found himself in a clearing under a dome of interlocking

101

hexagonal monkey bars. Isaiah was standing in the clearing, arms crossed and hair disheveled, his backpack hanging off one shoulder.

"I recognize you," said Isaiah. "What was your name again?"

"Tom," said Tom. "Jesus Christ, dude, my friend is fucking dead! He's fucking dead!"

"Who was your friend?" said Isaiah.

"Jordan. Oh fuck. Jordan is dead."

Isaiah nodded. He looked very tired. "The other three are dead too. Melissa, George..."
He closed his eyes for a moment. "There are other things in here. Things that aren't children. They come down from above and grab you and then they're gone again."

"We've been conned, man. This isn't a ladder to heaven. This is a fucking death trap."

Isaiah shook his head slowly. "God is testing us," he said.

"Bullshit," said Tom. "Jesus, dude, you look like you're about to pass out."

"I have to stay awake," said Isaiah. "I can't sleep or they'll take me."

"Who? What are these things?"

"I don't know. They move fast. One's bright red and one's blue. They crawl along the bars, really fast, and they blend in and they grab you when you're not looking."

Tom laughed. "This whole thing is so fucked. So fucked." He dropped his heavy backpack to the ground. "Here, I'll stay awake and keep watch, and you sleep. I slept not that long ago, I'm good. You look like you're

102

about to pass out."

Isaiah shook his head.

"For a couple hours at least," said Tom. "We can take turns. We're way better off together than alone, right man? Think about it. I don't know about you, but I don't want to be in here by myself. Especially not after that shit you just told me."

"You're probably right," said Isaiah.

"I am right. Lie down, I'll keep watch. If anything comes at us, I'll make noise and kick it and punch it and drive that fucker off. You just better do the same for me later on. Go to sleep."

"You can't," Isaiah said. "You can't fight them." He dropped his backpack and lay down on the rubber-padded ground, using the backpack as a pillow. "You can't..." he murmured.

Within a few minutes, he was asleep.

Tom sat down and stared up into the metal canopy. It was very quiet. He wished there were bird sounds. There was only the occasional slight hiss of the wind.

He sat for some time. He didn't have a watch. The light never changed. The only measure of time was the vague progression of his thoughts. He thought in tight circles, seeing Jordan's broken body over and over again and trying think about anything else. He thought about how trapped they were, how he had no idea where he was. Tight, panicked circles. He desperately wanted a drink or a hit. Though weed would probably just make it all worse. He wished he had a drink. Time was passing but he had no idea how much.

He remembered the vial of Milk and considered taking some but decided it was a bad idea. Some more time passed, and he remembered the vial of Milk again. He got it out. He held it and stared at it and thought in more panicked circles and wanted to do something. He had to change something to escape the endless looping. Jordan's broken body. Trapped. Lost. Dead body. He sucked some liquid into the dropper and very carefully put a drop on his tongue.

He wanted to calm down. He wanted to not feel anything, or care about anything. The Milk was bitter and slowly he felt his circling thoughts drift in and out of focus. And slowly they drifted and he couldn't really keep track of them. They lost their rhythm and fell into the hissing background and he couldn't keep track of them. Time was passing but each moment was the same. There was no change. Each was just the same. There was just this one moment forever, and that was everything, and Tom paid it no mind.

At some point Isaiah started screaming in his sleep, shattering Tom's still, crystalline moment.

"Hey," Tom grabbed his shoulder and shook him. "Hey, wake up. Stop screaming, man."

***

Samantha woke up with a headache in a place she didn't recognize. She was on a couch in an empty apartment.

"At least I'm indoors this time," she said.

The walls were all white and there was no sign of decoration. There was an armchair and a kitchen area with a bare counter. The rest of the room was empty. Her head really hurt.

She rolled onto her back and stared at the black box on the ceiling.

"I should probably leave," she said, but she didn't move.

The light through the window made a bright square on the wall that hurt her eyes.

"Hello again," said Lilith.

Samantha slowly pushed herself up onto her elbows.

"Hey," she said. "I remember you. What happened last night?"

"We got drunk," she said. She was standing in the doorway of the bedroom. "You got very drunk, so I brought you back to my home."

"That was nice of you," said Samantha. "I'm glad I didn't throw up on anything." She laughed at herself.

"I am glad too," said Lilith.

***

Later, they were sitting at the table eating generic cereal, the kind that came from the food dispensers. There was a lot of awkward silence.

"It's kind of empty in here," said Samantha.

Lilith was staring off into a corner. It took her a moment to look up and respond.

"You're right, probably," she said. "That's what I'm used to seeing. Everything in the city used to be like this. Empty like this. Now there's so much."

"So much what?" said Samantha.

Lilith laughed and made a sweeping gesture with her arm. "Everything! None of these things used to be here."

Samantha spooned more cereal into her mouth. It didn't taste great but eating made her feel less sick. "You were saying something about that last night. I don't get what you mean. When were things different?"

"I don't know. Not very long ago. Everything was different. Completely. Do you know about the computer?"

"Sure," said Samantha. "The computer made us, everyone knows that. Why?"

"But you think you grew up here? How long do you think you've been here?"

"Yeah, my whole life," said Samantha. "Twenty years or however long."

Lilith shook her head. "The computer is lying."

"Why?" said Samantha. "Why would it do that?"

"None of this was here," said Lilith. "Less than a year ago. The buildings were all empty. You could walk and not see anyone in the street. Your memories are not true."

"None of what you're saying is making sense right now," said Samantha. She was beginning to feel uncomfortable.

Lilith smiled at her sadly and offered her the cereal box. Samantha poured herself another bowl of cereal and poured milk on it. She picked up her spoon, then dropped it on the table and buried her face in her hands, gasping for air and struggling not to vomit.

"Are you ok?" Lilith had grabbed her arm.

"Yeah, it's just…." She couldn't finish. She focused on the black space behind her eyes and focused on taking deep, slow breaths. Gradually, the tremendous wave of nausea began to recede.

She put her palms down on the table, and opened her eyes.

"Fuck," she said, wiping the tears from her eyes.

"What's wrong? What happened?"

"Nothing," Samantha said. "Just felt sick there for a second. It was nice of you to let me stay here, I don't want to repay you by, you know, throwing up on everything." She gave Lilith a weak smile and went back to staring at her cereal bowl.

"You have a hangover," said Lilith.

"Just a little," said Samantha. "I don't know if I'm going to be able to eat the rest."

"It's ok. Here, I have something to help." Lilith pushed her chair back from the table and went into the bedroom. She came back with a small glass pipe.

"What is it?" said Samantha.

"It's a drug. It will make you feel better." She handed Samantha the pipe and a lighter.

"What drug? It looks like plant stuff."

"It is. They grow it up on the level above. Burn it and breathe in the smoke."

Samantha took a hit and coughed it out. "Level above?" she said. She remembered something from the day before, someone saying something about a lower level.

"You can go through the sky and there's another whole city up there. And I think there is another level above that one. It's like circles inside circles, who knows how many," Lilith said.

"Up through the sky?" Samantha managed to hold the smoke and exhale it carefully this time.

Lilith looked amused. "Yes. There's a building with an elevator in it. It takes you up really far too a cave. The sky is solid, you see? Like a dome. You go up through the cave and come out in this other city built

107

on top of the sky."

Samantha shook her head. "How much of this should I smoke?"

"Do one more," said Lilith. "I know you don't understand these things I'm saying, but they are true." She took the pipe and lighter from Samantha and took a hit herself.

"If you say so," said Samantha. She was beginning to feel light-headed. "Do you have any Milk?" she asked. "You know… 'Milk' Milk."

Lilith blew out a cloud of smoke. "No," she said. "It's bad for you. You shouldn't do that."

"Lots of things are bad for you," said Samantha. Her voice sounded strange. She could hear water running.

She came back suddenly to the present. She was lying on the couch. Lilith was washing dishes in the kitchen. Samantha laughed.

"What's funny?"

"My mind was wandering and I didn't even realize it," she said. "I was just remembering us having breakfast."

Lilith smiled at her over the counter. "Do you feel better now?"

"I think my head still kind of hurts, if I pay attention to it," said Samantha, "but only if I make myself pay attention to it."

"I think that's probably better. I told you it would work."

There was peculiar buzzing, droning sound. It hissed and twisted over itself like snakes. Lilith was sitting on the floor of the living room turning a crank on small red-painted speakerbox.

"What is that?"

"It's a music-making box. You make sounds by turning the crank. Want to try?"

"I think I'm fine where I am."

"Do you have a home, Samantha?"

"Not really. Do you need me to go?"

"No, I was just curious if you had somewhere to live."

"I live wherever. It's not too difficult, really."

Samantha was in the kitchen and she couldn't remember why. She opened the refrigerator door and closed it again.

"Do you want to do something with me?" said Lilith.

"Like what kind of thing?"

"Let's find out where these go."

Lilith was tracing out a path of the blue wire with her finger, following it out of the black box on the ceiling and going down the wall and out under the doorframe.

"Where the blue wires go?"

"Isn't it interesting to think about? Come with me."

The door closed behind them. Samantha squinted in the pale light. They were going down metal stairs into the parking lot of an apartment complex. All the buildings were white-washed and featureless.

"Come this way."

The blue wire came down from the apartment over the balcony. They followed it along the wall around several corners.

"I don't know this part of town," said Samantha.

Around the back of the building, the wire stretched up off the wall to a small pole and from there up to a tall metal electrical pole where it joined a tangle of other blue wires from other buildings. They followed the line down an alleyway and across the street.

"Do you know where we are?" said Samantha.

"No."

They passed a small robot collecting cans, just little metal boxes on wheels with a single arm. The buildings here looked rundown. Some were only partially built. They passed a large metal framework covered in tarps. One was just a façade with an empty lot behind it. She could see the sky and clouds through the empty window socket.

Up ahead, the street and sidewalk crumbled away into a wash like a river basin. Across the wash, there were fragmented islands of asphalt and buildings. The blue power lines stretched off into air above the rubble.

Samantha and Lilith were standing at the top of the wash, looking down.

"Do you want to keep going?" asked Lilith.

"I don't know," said Samantha. Her head was beginning to clear, but she felt disoriented and nervous.

"Come on, let's find where it goes."

"I don't understand, why does the city fall apart out here? I've never been anywhere like this."

Lilith laughed. "You've never been out this far? We can always follow the wires back."

Samantha imagined walking back, going through the old routine of scrounging up money and alcohol any way she could.

Lilith was tugging on her hand. "Come on."

***

The building-islands became smaller and less dense the farther out they went until finally there was nothing but flat sand and broken glass. The city receded behind them and in the distance up ahead they could see green grassy hills rising up from the plain. The line of utility poles continued on and on, becoming smaller and smaller and disappearing behind the hills. It was quiet except for a slight breeze and the crunching of glass beneath their shoes.

"We aren't really going to go all the way down there, are we?" said Samantha. She was mostly sober again and she could feel a dull pain beginning to creep back into her skull.

"Let's just go a little farther. We haven't been walking for very long. Not much more than an hour I think."

"Yeah, but, I mean," said Samantha, "we can see there's nothing up ahead for a really long way. The wires just keep going… Really? Just one hour? It seems like we're out in the middle of nowhere."

"Maybe two hours. You don't have anything you need to do, yes?" said Lilith.

"Well, not really. But what about food and stuff?"

"You're hungry again so soon?"

"Sort of. I don't know," said Samantha. "Mainly it's just this fucking hangover."

Lilith laughed. "You drank so much!"

"Yeah, no shit," said Samantha. "It tends to happen."

"Let's just go to the top of this big hill," said Lilith. "So we can see down the other side. Ok?"

Samantha sighed dramatically. "Fine…"

Lilith punched her in the arm.

"Ow! Quit it."

"I'm just playing!"

"Play less violently then."

"You know this is a fun adventure, admit it," said Lilith.

"I'd have more fun if you weren't hitting me."

"Aww," said Lilith, hugging Samantha with enough force that the two of them stumbled and nearly fell. "I'm sorry I hit you. Cheer up."

"Goddammit, Lilith. I hate non-hung-over people so much."

The ground was patchy with grass now and beginning to slant upwards. The air was moist and smelled like plants. The sky, pale grey in the city, was now bright blue. They topped the first small hill and headed down into a grassy valley.

"I don't think I've ever seen this much grass before," said Samantha.

"Me neither," said Lilith.

"You've never been out this far?"

"Not this far."

There was a succession of small hills and valleys, each hill slightly taller than the last and each valley slightly shallower. By the time they reached the base of the tallest hill, Samantha's headache had grown into a sick pulsing in the middle of her skull. As she slowed down, Lilith seemed to move proportionally faster, finally sprinting the last few meters to the top.

"Sam!" she said. "Come see!"

"I'm trying," said Samantha.

Lilith stood on top of the hill, pale skin, white hair and light grey clothing contrasting with the blue background. Samantha looked down at her feet and forcefully willed them to keep going, up and up, trying to ignore the growing queasiness in her stomach until she bumped into Lilith and looked up.

The valley below was crisscrossed with dirt paths and dotted with small dome-like houses. Scattered about haphazardly were colorful dinosaur statues, some toppled over, some half buried.

"Weird," said Samantha. "What is this place?"

"Come on, let's see if anyone is in the houses," said Lilith. She started off down the hill.

"You said just to the top of the hill!" said Samantha, but she was following.

The grass gave way to a path. They walked past an orange and blue stegosaurus, about the size of a person, half buried. Up close it looked shiny and fake, like it was made out of plastic. There was also a plastic wooly mammoth, about five feet long, tipped over on its side.

Lilith had run up to one of the houses and was knocking on its door. The house was like an igloo covered in khaki spackling, protruding from the side of a hill. Lilith was opening the door as Samantha caught up to her.

"It's unlocked," Lilith said.

"I can see that," said Samantha.

"Hello! Is anyone home?" Lilith called out. Her voice echoed back at them.

"Sounds big in there," said Samantha.

"It's stairs," said Lilith. "Hello! May we come in? Hello!" She walked inside and Samantha followed, glancing over her shoulder. There was no sign of life in the valley, just plastic dinosaurs, grass blowing in the breeze and the line of blue wires swaying overhead.

The house's front door opened directly to a staircase, spiraling downward into the ground. Everything inside the house was khaki-colored too. The stairway was lit by small circular lights on the walls. Leaving the door open behind her, Samantha followed Lilith down the stairs.

"Slow down, geez," said Samantha. Lilith had already disappeared around the curve of the tight spiral.

"Hello!" Lilith called. "Is anyone here? We are just visiting!"

Down below on the stairs to her right Samantha could see an open doorway. She paused at the doorway. She could hear Lilith's voice receding into the hollow spaces further below. The room through the doorway was white and round. There was no furniture. The floor was littered with colorful blown-glass cats of different shapes and sizes. Each had a differently colored head, body, tail and paws, bright reds and deep blues. Nearest to her was a cat with an elongated body like a balloon animal, cloudy white. It had a small blue bubble of a head on top with pointy glass ears. Samantha touched it gently with a finger and it liquefied, bouncing away from her touch. Startled, she jumped back. It rippled and jiggled like gelatin, its long body swaying back and forth in slow waves. Each wave was slightly smaller than the last and the vibrations gradually slowed to a stop and in an instant it was solid, just a blown-glass sculpture again.

"Samantha!" Lilith's voice sounded like it was

coming from the bottom of a well.

"What?" Samantha called back, still staring at the cat.

"Come here!"

"What is it?"

"Do you want food? There's food."

"Hell yes I do," said Samantha.

She left the cat room and continued down the stairs. A few flights down she passed another doorway. Through this one she could see a glass case like a fish tank sitting on a table in the middle of another blank room. The glass case had a small model sheep made out of cotton balls inside. It had wires stretching out to a large metal crank attached to the case. Samantha hesitated for a moment but continued on down the stairs.

She came to another doorway. Lilith was sitting at a table, opening a jar of mustard. There was a small refrigerator behind her and behind that a counter with a sink and a row of cupboards. On the floor next to Lilith was another glass cat, this one with a spherical body and a large ovular head.

"What took so long?" Lilith said. "Come have some food. I found mustard and bread."

Samantha took a seat across the table.

"Check this out," she said. "Touch the cat."

Lilith eyed the cat suspiciously. "Why?"

"Just see what happens."

Lilith picked up a butter knife and poked the cat with it, sending a pulse of concentric ripples across its body. She flinched back in surprise and started giggling.

"Weird, right?" said Samantha.

Lilith smeared mustard on pieces of bread and they

ate mustard and bread sandwiches.

"What time is it?" said Samantha. "We should probably go home soon."

"Why?"

"You said just to the top of the hill. What time is it now?"

"You don't have important things to do."

"Not really, no. I just kind of want to get back to the city."

"Why?" said Lilith. "What do you want to do there? You don't have a home, why can't this be home."

"This is someone else's home. We don't even know whose home it is." Samantha finished her piece of bread and smeared mustard on another. "Besides I kind of want a drink."

"You were sick because you drank so much, and now you want to drink more?"

"Or some Milk. Or I could smoke more of that stuff you had, that was cool. I just want something to make me be not sober, is what I mean."

"Why?"

"Jesus, you're like one of those little kids who keeps asking why to everything. I don't know, I don't like being sober for too long. It's this cycle. You wake up, you're sober for a little while, then you start unsobering yourself, then you get fucked up, then you go to sleep and then you wake up again. It just keeps going. It's like how you start out at home, then you go out on a journey somewhere, and then you come home again."

"But you're on a real journey!"

"Yeah, ok, maybe I'm ready to go home now. Maybe the not-sober part is really the coming home part.

116

It's like you wake up in the middle of a desert every morning and you slowly work your way home so you can pass out in your soft, safe bed. And then you wake up in the desert again."

"That sounds like a sad thing."

"I just want to feel like I'm doing something. Getting fucked up is doing something."

"We're doing something! We're exploring."

"I like exploring, sure," said Samantha. "But everywhere I go is kind of the same place because I'm still me. I'm sick of being me all the time."

Lilith shook her head. "You're only a few months old," she said.

Samantha looked at her funny but didn't say anything.

Lilith looked troubled. Then in an instant she was cheerful, like the sun swallowing a dark cloud. "Come on," she said. "Finish eating and then we'll keep exploring. If you're tired of being you, than stop doing the same thing that you are always doing. How is doing the same thing every day escaping from yourself? You're trapping yourself on purpose. This way you'll actually see something new. The more new things you see, the more you get to be new."

"I guess so," said Samantha. She reached for the mustard jar but it was empty.

***

"Wake up, idiot."

The voice sounded familiar. Everything was dark and numb, but sensations were creeping back in. He was lying on something uncomfortable.

"I'm alive again, aren't I," said Jordan. He opened

117

his eyes. He was sprawled out on the same web of metal as before, but this time he was in one solid piece. Far above him, he could see the monkey bars he'd fallen from.

"Very astute of you," said the voice. It seemed to be coming from everywhere and nowhere.

"You're talking to me inside my head aren't you?" said Jordan.

"Right again! I apologize for calling you an idiot, you are clearly a very clever little boy! Now stop wasting time and climb down from here."

Jordan looked down at his hands. The gash on his right palm had been replaced by smooth white material that looked more like dried glue than skin. He pressed his fingers against it. It was numb and felt like rubber.

"I've patched you up with the Milk in your body. There's a lot of it floating around in there, you know. It's in your blood. It's in your bones. It's in your brain. Have you figured out who I am yet?"

"The Olm," said Jordan. He gingerly tilted his head on its axes. His bones ached where they had been broken, but it was a dull pain. "Why did you bring me back to life? I thought you hated me."

The Olm laughed. "Of course not. You have hated me, perhaps. If you step on an ant it's because it happened to get underfoot, not because you hate it. How ridiculous it would be to hate an ant."

"So you brought me back to life so you can make fun of me inside my head, basically," said Jordan.

"No, that is merely an added benefit. I have brought you back to life because I'm going to help you get to the top."

"To the top of the New Equipment? Why would you do that?"

"I like helping. I'm a very generous person, is that so hard to believe?"

"Yes," said Jordan.

"Your hostility towards me is completely unfounded. What have I ever done to you?"

"You ruined my life."

"Oh really? I was selling you completely safe product. If you had continued to buy from me, nothing bad would have happened."

"You murdered me," said Jordan. "You gave me that pill and told me to swim in the Milk. You knew what would happen."

"You sure do talk a lot for a murder victim," said the Olm. "Besides, I didn't make you do any of that. Your girlfriend—"

"Don't talk about her," said Jordan.

"Do you want to know how she's doing by the way?"

"No," said Jordan. "Don't talk about her."

"Fine, fine. We have more important issues to deal with. The first of which is climbing down from here."

"Why are you helping me?" said Jordan.

"Because you're clearly too stupid to do it without help," said the Olm. "Look at you. You were killed by playground equipment."

"This place is a trap," said Jordan.

"Of course it is. The Reverend Timmy needs his amusement. Do you have any idea how boring it is to be a God? But while the Reverend is content to watch you idiots mill about and get yourselves killed, some of us

119

want to see actual plot development. Rising action. Climax. Denouement. All that good stuff."

"Where's Tom?"

"I'm going to guide you to him, don't worry. The first step is climbing down from here, like I keep telling you. It will be easier for both of us if you follow directions. You won't keep getting killed and I won't have to keep bringing you back to life like this."

Jordan looked around the not-day, not-night of his metal and plastic prison. Somewhere in the distance he heard a child scream. He began to climb down.

***

"Climb up the blue rope and take a right," said the Olm.

"Why do you want me to get to the top anyway?" said Jordan. "What's in it for you?"

"Don't you want to get to the top?"

"I don't know, what's up there?" Jordan climbed up the blue rope hand over hand, bracing his feet on the knots.

"Look, you don't have to do what I tell you," said the Olm. "You can do whatever you want."

"Why won't you tell me what's up there?"

"What I will tell you," said the Olm, "is that getting to the top is the only way you will ever get out of this place. No children ever leave the way they came in. You can try to find it, if you want. You can kill yourself, if you want, but I'll just keep bringing you back to life every time you die. You could grow up, live for eighty years and die an old man and I would bring you back again as a child. If you don't get to the top, you will be here for eternity."

"Won't you get sick of doing that over and over again?" Jordan pulled himself up on the platform and paused to catch his breath.

"I suspect you will get sick of it first," said the Olm. "Take a right, then keep going straight until you see a green stairway."

Jordan started walking. A tangle of rainbow-colored barbed wire hung low overhead. A tiny white jellyfish flew past his face and he waved it away. The path twisted and weaved but it did not branch. Jordan ran his hand along the crisscrossing metal bars that walled in the sides.

"You'll tell me if there's any more traps, right?" said Jordan.

"Of course. The good Reverend may be amused by such trivial tortures but for me, watching stupid children die loses its novelty pretty quickly. Don't worry, the barbed wire is for children who fall from above. As you'll soon see."

"What is that supposed to mean?" Jordan rounded a curve into a cloud of floating white jellyfish. He stumbled back, waiving them away from his face. "Fuck!"

"They aren't interested in you, you aren't bleeding," said the Olm.

In the middle of the cloud, a small, pale hand dangled down from the barbed wire. Blood was streaked down the arm, mostly dried, but some still dripped from the fingertips. The jellyfish swarmed around and clustered on the bloodied hand.

Jordan stared. "I think I'm going to throw up," he said.

"That would be silly," said the Olm, "especially because you don't have any food or water. Keep going, we're getting close to your friends."

Jordan crouched down and pressed himself against the wall, inching his way past the cloud of jellyfish. The hand hung motionless, pointing the way down like a plumb-line. Above it in the rainbow wire there was more bloodied flesh and torn fabric. Jordan saw an open eye and looked away quickly.

"Oh come on," said the Olm. "You used to clean up dead bodies for a living!"

"Yeah, well, back then I didn't know what it felt like," said Jordan.

He crawled around another curve and the wall of bars ended abruptly in open space, bisected diagonally by something like fire escape stairs, but green and coated with rubber. Jordan stood up and peered out around the wall. The stairway stretched both up and down at a constant angle, intersecting with numerous platforms and walkways. Beneath the steps there was nothing, just a straight drop.

"Don't fall or you'll die again and we'll have to climb all the way back up," said the Olm.

Holding on to the wall for support, Jordan climbed up awkwardly onto the stairs and started walking down. The drop was visible in the spaces between the steps. It made him dizzy.

"Get off on the platform here," said the Olm.

"Yeah, one level down, I got it."

***

"Tom!" Someone was shaking him. "Tom, get up. Someone's coming."

Tom bolted upright. Everything was fuzzy. He couldn't quite remember where he was.

"Huh?" he said.

"Someone's coming through that plastic tube," said Isaiah. "I can hear footsteps."

Tom remembered where he was.

"Shit," he said. "Goddamn it."

"It might be a friend," said Isaiah, "but be ready."

"This place hasn't been super friendly so far," said Tom. He reached into his pocket and pulled out his fork. Isaiah kept his butter knife tucked in his belt, but rested a hand on it. "I guess we— oh Jesus fuck!"

Isaiah went tense.

"Hi Tom," said Jordan from the mouth of the plastic tunnel. He eyed Isaiah. "Who's this kid? You look kind of familiar."

"Oh fuck this," said Tom.

"Do you know him?" said Isaiah.

"Yeah I fucking know him, he's dead," said Tom. "It's gotta be a trick or some shit."

"I was dead, and now I'm alive again," said Jordan. "Are you really that shocked?"

"Uh, yeah," said Tom. "I saw you down there. You were fucked up. Your head was like..." his voice shook, "dangling..."

Jordan rubbed his neck. "Yeah, I know," he said. "I got fixed with Milk."

"I remember you now," said Isaiah. "You were on the bus."

"Yeah that's right," said Jordan.

"Bullshit," said Tom. "It's a trick or something. How do I know it's really you?"

123

"I don't know," said Jordan. "We already argued about that, remember? Cocoons and butterflies? I don't know if I'm the same as the last time I died or the time I died before that, but I have all the same memories."

"I can't believe you're alive, man," said Tom. "It's like one of those dreams that's too good to be true, like you're sitting on your grandmas lap and then you wake up and remember that she died twenty years ago and now you're a loser."

"Well, this isn't a dream," said Jordan. "I don't think it is, anyway. I mean, I feel like I'm here. But you're right, it is too good to be true and it probably is a trap. I have voices in my head now."

"What kind of voices?" said Isaiah. "Holy or demonic?"

"Pretty sure the second one," said Jordan. "It's just one voice, really. The Olm is talking to me in my head now. He's giving me directions. He told me how to find you guys."

"The Olm?" said Tom.

"Oh thank God!" said Isaiah. "What did he say? What does he want?"

"He wants to help me get to the top. Or us, I guess," said Jordan.

"He does?" said Tom.

"Don't you see? It's a miracle!" said Isaiah. "The Olm has risen you from the dead so that you might come back and help us find the path to salvation! I knew it all had to be a test! Despite everything, I kept strong my faith!"

"Don't get too excited," said Jordan. "Like I said, it's got to be some kind of trap. I don't know what's waiting for us at the top, but it can't be good. The Olm doesn't help people."

"What? What do you mean?" said Isaiah.

"The Olm," said Jordan. "He's evil and I don't know what he wants, but he wants us to suffer. I know that much."

Isaiah's face contorted with rage. "You can't… How…"

"Ok, dude," said Tom. "I am really fucking confused right now. You're alive again. But the Olm is talking to you in your head. And he's evil."

"Antichrist!" shrieked Isaiah. "False prophet!" He drew his butter knife and held it with the blade below his fist. Jordan flinched back. Tom grabbed Isaiah by the arm and pulled him back.

"Everyone calm the fuck down!" said Tom.

"Is that a butter knife?" said Jordan.

"How do you know the Olm is evil?" said Tom.

"I've known he was evil this entire time, man," said Jordan. "I've been telling you that."

"Yeah, but you never had a good reason," said Tom. "Do you have a good reason now? He brought you back to life, right?"

"Yeah, but… he's just an asshole. He's always been an asshole and his voice in my head sounds like an asshole too." Jordan looked off to one side, irritated. "Shut up," he said.

"Dude… if what you're saying is true, and you're not some evil robot copy of you, than it sounds like the Olm saved your life."

"A miracle!" snarled Isaiah.

"Look, I could be an evil robot. I have no idea. All

I know is, I died, then I woke up, then the Olm told me how to find you guys. Maybe I'm a robot with my memories implanted and I'm programmed to betray you at any moment. How would I know? I'm just telling you what happened, and I think it's a trick or something, and I think we need to be careful."

"How dare you," said Isaiah.

"Man, calm your shit already," said Tom. "I think Jordan or possible robot Jordan is right. We'll let him guide us to the top, but we'll be careful. I think if being here for however long I've been here has taught me anything, it's that we need to be fucking careful. Jordan, come on over here."

Jordan started walking towards them. Tom met him halfway and hugged him.

"I'm glad you're not dead, man," Tom said. "Even if you are a robot."

"Yeah, me too," said Jordan.

***

"Wake up, your holiness."

The Reverend Timmy opened his eyes. He was lying on clean white sheets, dressed in clean white pajamas. The Olm was standing over him.

"I don't remember going to bed," said Rev. Timmy.

"Well, you didn't exactly 'go' to bed," said the Olm, "so much as you were carried there."

Rev. Timmy sat up. "Huh. Did I black out or something?"

"In a certain sense, yes," said the Olm. "You overdosed on heroin and died."

"Damn," said Rev. Timmy. "Again?"

The Olm nodded.

"Damn," said Rev. Timmy. "I don't even feel weird."

"Of course not," said the Olm. "Your servants cleaned you up quite well. They're getting good at it."

Rev. Timmy stared down at his toes. The toes of a child.

"Do you think I'm doing heroin too much?" he said.

"That is entirely up to you, of course," said the Olm. "As you are well aware, there are no physical consequences for anything you do. The Will to Power Converter will never let you come to any harm."

Rev Timmy reached up and touched the silver dot on his forehead.

"I know," he said. "What about consequences that aren't, like, physical? Like my emotions and stuff?"

The Olm shrugged. "The Will to Power converter can take care of that too, if you'd like."

Rev. Timmy shook his head. "I don't feel good about messing with my own brain like that."

"I might humbly point out that heroin messes with your brain too," said the Olm.

"Do you think I'm doing too much? Do you want me to stop?"

"I have no opinion, your Holiness. I want you to do what you want. I want you to fulfill your every desire. That is why I gave you the Converter to begin with. Never forget that you are a God, Timmy. You answer to no one, and that includes me. You could wish me dead at a whim and it would be so."

"Don't say shit like that. I would never do that. But can I ask for advice though?" said Rev. Timmy. "Do you think I should stop shooting up so much?"

The Olm tilted his eyeless pink head. "Well, your Holiness, perhaps if you feel the need to ask the question then you already have your answer."

Rev. Timmy thought about this. "Yeah, I guess that makes sense. Maybe I'll stop for a while. And then, sometime later, maybe I'll do it again if I feel like it. I don't have to stop forever."

"That sounds very sensible," said the Olm. "Now, if you're feeling better, perhaps you could address the congregation today? It's been a while, I worry that they may begin to grow restless."

"Sure, good point," said Rev. Timmy. "They're a bunch of stupid kids, someone needs to keep them in line." He swung his legs over the side of the bed. "They need me," he said. "They're lost without me."

"I will summon your servants for you," said the Olm.

"Is it true that I could just will myself to be happy?" said Rev. Timmy. "And I'd be happy? Just like that?"

"Of course!" said the Olm. "The Will to Power Converter has absolutely no limits. The universe is your clay to mold, Reverend, with a thought. Your brain is a part of that universe and your brain is you."

Rev. Timmy shook his head. "It's so weird to think about."

"It is 'weird', isn't it? The world that we live in," said the Olm.

Rev. Timmy climbed out of bed and headed for his wardrobe. "Why did you give me the dot anyway?" said Timmy. "Why didn't you just keep it for yourself?"

"Me? I wouldn't know what to do with it. Shall I summon your servants now?"

"Yeah, sure," said Rev. Timmy. "And have someone bring me an ice cream sundae."

***

Deep in a poorly-lit section of the New Equipment, Eenee and Oonoo hung upside-down from the monkey bar canopy, their foot-long toes coiled around the metal like tentacles. Eenee was holding a half-eaten dead child, wrapped up in his flexible fingers. He was peeling flesh off the child's face with his inflexible, muppet-like mouth. Eenee was red and Oonoo was blue. Their skin was slightly fuzzy soft plush.

"Eeneeneenee?" said Eenee, holding out the dead child in offering.

"Oonoonoonoo," said Oonoo, declining the offer.

Their black plastic pupils rolled and goggled aimlessly in the clear plastic of their eyes.

It was quiet in the Equipment. The only sound was Eenee's quiet, wet chewing and the soft dripping of blood and loose bits of flesh.

Then there was a scuffling of tennis shoes. Both plush heads snapped up at the sound. Below them on the platform, a child had darted out from behind a rideable frog on a spring and was sprinting towards the ball pit.

"Oonoonoo!" said Oonoo and dropped from the monkey bars. His muppet body hit the platform with a soft thud and he scuttled towards the child, his long-fingered hands flailing against the platform like squids out of water, propelling his misshapen body forward quickly but awkwardly.

The child leapt from the edge of the platform into the ball pit. He landed with a crunch and began to thrash forward. The plastic balls shifted and cascaded around him, their normally bright colors made dark and dull by the dim lighting. He tried to swim, but found he couldn't. Panting and struggling, he couldn't tell if he was moving forward at all. Plastic balls shifted under his kicking feet and he found himself slipping downwards.

Something came slithering up from beneath and behind him at incredible speed and something whipped around his leg and squeezed. He managed one scream before another tendril lashed around his neck and cut off his air supply.

Oonoo coiled the rest of his fingers around the boy and squeezed and squeezed.

"Oonoonoo," he burbled, "Oonoonoonoo."

The child's struggles began to weaken and slow.

"Oonoonoonoo... Oooonoonoonoonoo."

After a few minutes, the child was still. Oonoo wrapped him in the toes of one foot and wriggled his way through the balls back to the edge of the platform.

"Eeneenee!" Eenee greeted him as he surfaced.

"Oonoo," said Oonoo.

He climbed back up the monkey bars and began to eat.

***

"I don't feel too great," said Samantha.

"Why is it that you feel bad?" said Lilith. "Still the hangover?" She was a few meters away, standing on her tiptoes to reach a glassy fruit dangling from a tree. It was bright red and translucent, like a stained glass ornament. The light through the leaves was spotty and tinted green. They had left the grassy hills and houses and followed the blue wires to this place, a glass orchard. The sandwiches had made Samantha feel better at first, but she had begun to feel worse and worse since then.

"I don't know," said Samantha, "I feel kind of shaky. And weak. My head hurts. I really want a drink, like, really bad."

Lilith jumped and snagged the fruit. The tree leaves clattered against each other in a tinkley cascade . "Aha!" she said. "Do you want to go back to the city so you can drink?" She sniffed the fruit.

Samantha pressed her back up against a tree trunk. It was smooth and cold. The tree trunks were also glass but solid, a dark brown that was almost opaque. She slid to the ground and drew her knees up under her chin.

"I don't know," she said. "I sort of do, but at the same time the thought of going back there is really depressing. Back to the same old routine." She shook her head. "This place is amazing, I've never seen anything like it. I want to go further and see more."

Lilith took a small bite of the fruit, then a larger bite. She made a happy sound.

"I just wish I didn't feel like shit so I could enjoy it," said Samantha.

"Sam! Samsamsam!" said Lilith. "Try these fruits!"

"Is it good?" said Samantha. "They don't even look edible, they look like decorations."

"It is very edible, come try a taste!"

Samantha groaned and rested her head on her knees. "Maybe in a bit," she said.

Lilith held the half-eaten fruit in her cupped hands and came over to Samantha's tree. Red juice trickled down her arms and dripped from her fingers.

"Here! Try!" she said.

"You're making a mess," said Samantha. Lilith crouched down and pushed the fruit towards Samantha's face. "Stop! You're going to get it on me!"

"Just have a bite, you'll feel better," said Lilith.

Samantha rolled her eyes and took a bite from the fruit. It was juicy and delicious.

"It is pretty good," she said.

"See?" said Lilith.

Samantha wiped her face with her hands and slid down the tree trunk and sprawled out on the grass.

"Oh come on," said Lilith. "Get up. Eat some more of the fruit."

"Can't I just lie here a second?" said Samantha.

"It is so strange," said Lilith. "This place is not very far from the city. Here it is beautiful and there is food to eat. But the people in the city never come here. We are the only ones."

"If everyone came out here they'd just ruin it," said Samantha.

"Maybe," said Lilith.

Samantha lay on her back with her eyes closed. The grass underneath her was soft and cool. Light flashed in her eyelids at random as the wind rustled the leaves above her.

"The city people are made for the city," said Lilith. Her voice sounded further away now. "They are only a few months old so they don't know how to do anything else. You were made too, Sam. That's why you want to go back. You weren't built to leave."

"I like it here," said Samantha, "I just wish there was booze."

"I hope I didn't do the wrong thing," said Lilith.

Samantha tried to say something but her mind was wandering. She couldn't pin down a thought. She could see pictures in the flashing lights. Lilith was saying something but it sounded very far away.

"Lilith," said Samantha. "Don't leave. Don't leave me here."

She wanted to get up but she couldn't. She kept imagining getting up over and over again but she was still lying flat.

She felt like she was floating in space and spinning very fast.

She dreamed about the color yellow.

She woke up shaking and sweating. She squinted against the sunlight.

"Lilith!" she said.

A cool hand touched her forehead.

"You feel too hot," said Lilith. "Why are you crying?"

"Don't leave me here alone," said Samantha. She squeezed her eyes shut and felt tears leak out.

"I won't leave," said Lilith.

"I don't feel right," said Samantha. "Please talk to me about something."

"This will be over," said Lilith. "Wait. Please wait and don't worry. You will feel better when time passes. I'm going to get some more fruit for you."

"No, please stay with me," said Samantha. "I don't want to be by myself."

"I'm still here, I'm not going far."

"Don't go," said Samantha.

She felt like she was bobbing up and down in water.

She felt her head lift from the ground. Something sweet and wet was poured into her mouth.

"Drink the juice," said Lilith. "Carefully, don't breathe it."

Samantha drank until the thin trickle stopped. Her head was back on the grass.

"I don't know what else I can do," said Lilith. "Poor child."

"Just stay," said Samantha.

"Go back to sleep," said Lilith. "I won't leave you alone. You will feel better when you sleep and wake up again. I'm right next to you."

The computer made us for this, Samantha thought, but she couldn't speak.

The computer made you to help me and me to need you because that is what the computer needs, she thought.

Lilith was saying something she couldn't hear as she fell asleep.

***

Samantha woke up. Her eyes had been open for a while before she realized she was awake, staring up into the trees. The glass leaves swirled above her. They sounded like brittle wind chimes.

Samantha pushed herself up onto her elbows with weak arms. Lilith was sitting with her back to a tree not far away. She looked worried.

"Samantha," Lilith said. "How do you feel?"

Samantha groaned. "Well at least I'm conscious," she said. "That's got to be a good sign. How long was I out?"

Lilith shrugged. "It's always light here," she said. "It seems to be. The city used to be like this too, just light all the time."

"Can I have some more of that fruit?" said Samantha.

Lilith moved into a crouch and began to rummage through a small knapsack. She pulled out a clear plastic bag with radial slices of clear red fruit.

"Where did you get all that stuff?" said Samantha.

"There is another house," said Lilith. "A little ways through the trees. Like before, no one lives there. I made more sandwiches there, do you want a sandwich?"

"Maybe later," said Samantha. "Let's not get too crazy just yet. I'm really thirsty."

Lilith stood up and brought her the baggie of fruit. She helped Samantha sit up and rotate to rest her back on the tree while they ate.

Samantha took a tentative bite, then devoured the slice, then two slices at once. "God, so good," she said.

"I told you!" said Lilith. "Didn't I?"

"And you were not wrong," said Samantha. She ate another slice. Lilith still looked a little worried but she was smiling now. "What do you mean when you talk about how the city was before?" said Samantha. Lilith's smile faltered and she looked a little more worried. "Come on, I want to know. When was it day all the time there?"

Lilith sighed. "Only a few months earlier," she said. "I'm not sure the exact time."

"Why don't I remember that then? It's been normal, night and day, night and day, my whole life."

"That's what I was trying to explain." Lilith chewed on her lower lip, her eyes shifting down and to the left. "The city was empty then. There were a few people, but not many. Maybe you were there and I didn't see you, but probably not if you don't remember."

"So where was I back then?" said Samantha.

Lilith shook her head. "I don't know. I think you and the rest of the people are new. You were just made like you were already old."

"So, like, all my memories of before then are fake?" said Samantha.

Lilith shrugged.

"That's so weird," said Samantha.

"What do you remember from before?" said Lilith.

"I don't know," said Samantha. "Just… the routine, mainly. Get money. Spend it on booze and drugs and try to get more money again."

"Nothing else?" said Lilith. She continued to nibble her lower lip with her sharp teeth. "Do you remember how you were when you were a child?"

Samantha thought for a moment. "I guess not. I never really thought about it."

"You don't remember being made in a tube?" said Lilith. "The robots?"

"What? Robots? All that sounds completely nuts to me," said Samantha.

"But you don't remember how it was?"

Samantha shook her head. "I never think about it," she said. "I just kind of feel like I've lived my whole life. I feel like I have some backstory, like it's there somehow, but if I actually try to remember something that happened to me back then, I can't. Everything in the city was just… really familiar. It was opposite of new, it was boring."

They were quiet for a moment.

"Man," said Samantha, "I was made already bored. That's fucked up."

Lilith laughed.

"Isn't that fucked up? I didn't even get a chance to get bored on my own."

"Yes," said Lilith, smiling.

"Can I have a sandwich now?" said Samantha. "I kind of want a sandwich."

***

After eating some food and resting in the shade of the glass trees, Lilith took Samantha to the house she had found. It was another dome, but larger than the earlier houses had been and made out of white frosted glass with four glass foyers stretching out at right angles. In the center of the dome was a spiral staircase leading down. Above their heads, suspended by wires of different lengths, hundreds of colorful glass butterflies hung motionless in space.

They took the stairs down to the kitchen where Samantha made a sandwich for herself from logo-less packages of lunch meats and rubbery cheeses. There was a pitcher of bright red juice in the fridge. They each poured themselves a glass. It tasted the same as the fruit from outside but sweeter and more condensed. It tasted like the color red.

Further down the stairway there was a small room with two cots. The walls, ceiling and floor were smooth and painted blue. Lilith explained that there were more rooms like this, each with walls of a different color. All of the items in each room were exactly the same color as the walls. The next one down was a pale green. The next one was cyan. Samantha sat down on one of the blue cots in the blue room.

"I wish there was a way to turn the lights off," she said. "I can't even tell where the light is coming from down here. Everything's just kind of lit."

"Do you want to sleep again?" said Lilith.

"Kinda," said Samantha. "I still feel kind of shaky and weak. The food helped though."

"I will sleep too," said Lilith.

"You don't have to if you don't feel like it," said Samantha. "I'm good, you can do whatever."

"I was worried for you," said Lilith. "When I'm worried I get tired."

Samantha looked down at her fingers. "Yeah I guess you probably were," said Samantha. "I'm sorry I was so, like, weird and needy before. It's kind of embarrassing."

"It's ok," said Lilith. She pressed on the cot's springy fabric to test it before climbing in and lying down. She lay on her side and curled her arm under her head. Samantha watched her and didn't move. Lilith looked up at her. "Come on," she said. "Let's sleep for a little time and then we can keep going when we wake up."

Samantha pulled her feet up onto the cot. "Wish there was a pillow," she said. She stared up at the blue ceiling. The color was completely even with no light or dark patches. It saturated her vision and left a yellow afterimage when she blinked. She could hear Lilith's breathing begin to slow.

"I was thinking," she said, "if I've only been alive for a few months, then you're the only friend I've really ever had."

"Mm," said Lilith. She sounded half asleep. "I had one other friend."

"Yeah?" said Samantha.

"Yes," said Lilith. "On the surface. But not for very long."

"Why not?"

"I didn't know him very much and then he died," said Lilith. "But we were friends for a little while."

"Oh," said Samantha. "I'm sorry. How did he die?"

Lilith took a deep breath and let it out slowly. "There was someone else," she said, "who I thought was my friend, but he wasn't. And he killed my friend."

"Oh," said Samantha. "That's fucked up. I'm sorry, Lilith."

"It's ok," said Lilith. "You're here now. I'm glad you're here with me, Sam."

"Me too," said Samantha.

"Try to sleep."

***

"Wait," said Isaiah. He stopped in his tracks.

Tom grabbed Jordan's arm and pulled him back. "What? What is it?"

Jordan looked down at Tom's hand with a blank expression.

"I recognize this place," said Isaiah.

"How?" said Tom. "It's just more goddamn monkey bars and shit. Everything looks the same around here."

"No, I remember this," said Isaiah. He pointed with a trembling finger. "That ladder." A green ladder hung down from the canopy in front of them. One of the handholds was broken. "It broke when Melissa tried to climb it. She…" his voice started to shake. "She fell down… she got cut..."

"Sounds familiar," said Jordan.

"What happened? Did she die?" said Tom.

"No, no," said Isaiah, "not yet. But this is the way we came before…"

Jordan turned to keep walking.

"No!" shouted Isaiah. "I'm not going back!"

Jordan stopped and sighed. "We have to go this way," he said.

"According to what? According to that devil voice?" said Isaiah.

"You mean the Olm?" said Jordan.

"Don't you see it's tricking you?" said Isaiah. "It's not really the Olm. It's a trick, you fool! It's the devil trying to lure us into a trap!"

"Look," said Jordan. "Yes, the voice is probably evil. And yes, those two… things are probably down there. It kind of makes sense, doesn't it? There are more traps if you're on the right path, it's just designed that way. But the Olm wants us to get to the top. I don't know why, but that's the whole reason it brought me back to life."

"So then? What's the plan? What does the 'Olm,'" Isaiah said the word with intense sarcasm, "say about getting past those god-forsaken monsters? What is the big plan."

Jordan cocked his head for a moment, listening. "He says we should use you as bait," he said. "And sneak past while they're busy eating you."

Isaiah stared at him for a moment his fists clenched and face reddening. Then he threw down his back pack and sprinted at Jordan. Tom jumped back out of the way. Isaiah hit Jordan low with his shoulder and they both went down.

"The fuck!" said Tom.

Isaiah rolled to the top and began to rain punches down on Jordan's face. Jordan struggled to cover his head with his arms.

"Goddamn it, stop!" said Tom. He grabbed Isaiah in a headlock and dragged him backwards. Isaiah flailed and kicked at the air. "Fucking quit!" said Tom. "Calm the fuck down! Isaiah! Fucking calm down, dude!"

Jordan lay on the ground with his arms over his face.

Isaiah snarled and thrashed.

"Dude," said Tom. "I'm not letting go until you stop. I will choke you unconscious if I need to. Fucking. Quit."

Isaiah went limp with a sob of rage, He tugged at Tom's arm and struggled to say something. Tom let go and dropped Isaiah to the ground. He sat there, red-faced and panting.

"I didn't say we were going to follow that plan," said Jordan. "That's just what he told me."

"Liar," said Isaiah.

"Jesus Christ, dude, let him talk," said Tom.

Jordan pushed himself up into a sitting position. "I just repeated what I heard," said Jordan. His teeth were bloody from a split lip. "But we're not going to do that. I'm going to be the decoy."

"Wait what?" said Tom.

"Don't you understand? I'm invincible," said Jordan. "The Milk in my body keeps healing me. Even if they kill me, I'll just keep coming back to life."

Jordan slowly climbed to his feet. He wiped the blood off his lips. The split had sealed itself shut. It was just a white line.

"You don't know for sure," said Tom. "What if you can only come back to life a limited number of times?"

"So?" said Isaiah.

"Shut the fuck up, man," said Tom.

Jordan shook his head. "The Olm says he won't let me die. He says the only way I can get out of here is if I get to the top. I can't kill myself, and those muppet things can't kill me. At least not forever."

"They'll eat you alive," said Isaiah, "just like my friends. I heard them screaming and screaming…"

Jordan shrugged. "It's not that hard to ignore pain if you know you're invincible," he said. "I'm kind of getting used to it."

"No way, dude, this is insane," said Tom. "There has to be another way. You don't want your guts getting ripped out by some fucking muppets, that does not sound like a good time."

"Well, we aren't going to kill them with forks and butter knives," said Jordan. "So if you can think of another way, let me know."

He started walking again.

"Wait, man!" said Tom. He looked at Isaiah.

Isaiah shrugged. "We're certainly better off with an invincible person on our team," he said. "Maybe it is a miracle after all."

"Yeah, you seem to be pretty flip-floppy on that," said Tom. "And if he's on our 'team' then start acting like he's on our team. Stop being an asshole."

"I'm sorry," said Isaiah. "It's just that my friends died and they didn't come back. Your friend came back

and I don't understand it. I know it's not his fault but…
it's just not fair."

"Yeah, shit's fucked up, isn't it?" said Tom.

"I'd give anything to see them again," said Isaiah.

Tom helped Isaiah to his feet. "That still doesn't
mean you get to be an asshole," he said. He called after
Jordan: "Slow down, dude! Wait for your goddamn
team!"

***

"You just love being a martyr, don't you," said the
Olm's disembodied voice.

Jordan didn't respond. He was sitting on a teeter-
totter, resting back on the slanted board with his feet on
the handle. Tom and Isaiah slept a few meters away,
using their backpacks as pillows.

"Maybe 'martyr' isn't the right word," said the
Olm. "You just like feeling sorry for yourself, and when
you die you get to feel sorriest of all. You get to
imagine people feeling sad about it. You picture it like
some tragic scene in a play, don't you? But guess what,
my boy, there's no audience."

"It would be stupid to let some other kid die who
won't come back," said Jordan. "It doesn't make sense."

"We'll see if you still feel that way when those
muppets tear the flesh from your bones," said the Olm.
"There's no guarantee that they'll bother to kill you first.
They might just start eating."

"Can't hurt worse than getting dissolved," said
Jordan.

"Well, I guess you'll get to find out, won't you? Be
sure to let me know."

"Why do you even care?" said Jordan.

"It takes time to get torn apart," said the Olm, "and then more time to put you back together again. If I have a fault, I suppose it's that I can be a little short on patience."

"But you'd be ok with me living in here until I die of old age," said Jordan. "You could just wait out that eighty years no problem."

The Olm laughed. Jordan subconsciously expected it to echo or reverberate like the movies, but it was short and dry. "Eighty years? You'd die of hunger a little sooner than that. And you'd die of thirst even sooner."

"So? I'd just come back again," said Jordan. "You didn't really think this through, did you?"

"If you want to spend the rest of eternity dying of thirst over and over again, be my guest," said the Olm. "I can find a different child for this task."

"I don't think any of them are Milk addicts, so that wouldn't work either," said Jordan.

"My, such attitude! I can't imagine the level of cognitive dissonance required for you to think that you're smarter than me after making so very many stupid decisions," said the Olm. "Do you want to know what your girlfriend is doing right now?"

"Don't talk about her," said Jordan.

"She never took the pill, you know."

"Shut up!"

The Olm went quiet. Jordan heart was racing. He felt sick to his stomach.

"Do you have any idea how creepy you sound?" said Tom from where he lay on the ground.

"Sorry," said Jordan. "I was trying to be quiet."

"It's not a volume problem. It's more of a 'talking

to yourself like a crazy person' problem," said Tom.

"I guess that makes sense," said Jordan.

"Want to switch? I feel pretty good, I can keep watch."

"I don't feel like sleeping."

Tom stood up and adjusted his dirty clothes. "Come on," he said. "Just lie down for a while and see how you feel after a few minutes. You're acting crazy enough already, it'll probably be worse if you're sleep-deprived too."

As his anger began to fade into a dull nausea, Jordan began to feel the weariness dragging him down like cement shoes. "Yeah, ok," he said. He climbed down from the teeter totter and Tom took his place.

Jordan laid his head down on the backpack and fell asleep.

***

The Reverend Timmy awoke to the sound of his phone ringing and a woman sobbing.

His head and neck hurt, so he willed them not to hurt, and they stopped hurting.

He opened his eyes. A woman was sitting on his bed crying, tapping frantically on the screen of his ringing cellphone.

"It's not going to work for you," said Timmy.

The woman screamed and threw the phone at him. It flew over him and hit the wall above his head.

"Goddamn it, don't do that," said Timmy, sitting up. There was something around his neck. A belt. He reached up and loosened it.

"Oh my god," said the woman. "Oh my god."

"What? Calm down. Or… shut up at least," said

Timmy.

"You weren't breathing," said the woman. "I thought…"

"Yeah, I was probably dead," said Timmy. "It happens."

"I thought I killed you," she sobbed.

"Like I said, it happens," said Timmy.

The phone made a "new voicemail" sound, then started ringing again.

"You told me to keep going," she said.

"Don't worry about it." Timmy reached down behind the bed, searching for his phone.

"I'm so sorry. I knew I was being too rough. Oh god…"

"I would've told you if you were too rough," said Timmy. "You did good. Don't worry about it. And please, for fucks sake, stop crying." His fingers touched vibrating plastic.

"You were all purple. And you weren't breathing. And I couldn't open the door…"

Timmy fished his phone out from behind the bed.

"And I tried screaming for help, but no one came," she said.

Timmy unlocked his phone and put it to his ear. "Hello hello," he said. "What? What's so goddamn important."

"I'm sorry, am I disturbing you?" It was the Olm's voice.

"I want to go home," said the woman.

"You aren't fucking disturbing me," said Timmy. "Just tell me what the fuck it is."

"You might want to get down to the viewing

146

station," said the Olm. "Entertainment is imminent."

"Oh yeah?" said Timmy. "What is it? The muppets?"

"Indeed," said the Olm. "You'd better hurry. They're getting close."

"Shit," said Timmy. He ended the call and speed-dialed "1." "Hey, Clarissa, can I get some staff in here? I need… clothes. And… cocaine. And money. Quickly, please!"

He ended the call and tossed the phone down on his bed, unbuckling the belt from around his neck. The woman was curled up on the floor with her face buried in her hands, crying.

Timmy sighed. "Everything's ok now, you see?" he said. "I'm alive again. I'm about to pay you and send you on your way."

She didn't reply.

"You were so tough last night, I'm kind of disappointed. Or whenever it was. How long was I dead? Never mind, doesn't matter. Jesus Christ, perk up a bit would you? Let me see that smile…"

"Fuck you," she said.

"That's more like it," said Timmy.

The door opened and three women in tuxedos came in. One was carrying a child-sized business suit and a pair of pajamas. Another was carrying a golden platter of cocaine. The third helped the crying woman to her feet and pressed a roll of bills into her palm. The woman hugged her and began crying into the shoulder of her tuxedo.

The woman with the clothes and the woman with the cocaine stood at attention at the foot of the bed.

Timmy gestured for the latter. The platter was held under his nose and he was handed a straw. The lines were already cut. Timmy put the straw to his nose and snorted one vigorously. He sniffed in deeply, rubbing his nose.

"Do you want any?" he said. "Do you think she wants any cocaine? Ah, fuck it, she's not paying attention. Go on, get her out of here. Give her extra money or something. And from now on you guys are allowed to unlock the door if the girl starts screaming about me being dead or any of that shit. This is not the kind of shit I need to deal with right when I come back to life."

The woman in the tuxedo awkwardly guided the crying woman to the door.

Timmy did a line with the other nostril and gestured for the other woman to bring him the clothing. He chose the pajamas.

"Someone get a bowl of popcorn ready," he said.

***

"Come on, dude," said Tom. "It's a fucking merry-go-round."

Tom was kneeling on the merry-go-round with one leg, pushing off the ground with the other to make it spin.

"How is that something you want to do right now?" said Jordan. He sat down on a tire swing nearby and dropped his backpack to the rubber-padded ground. He wasn't sure how much he'd actually slept, but his body felt heavy and his thoughts were slow and muddy.

"Are you sure we're going the right way?" said Isaiah. "I don't remember any of this."

Jordan shrugged. "We're going the way the Olm is telling me to go."

"So… straight into a deathtrap then," said Isaiah. "Great."

"Seriously, guys. This is shit is fun," said Tom.

Jordan stared down at his dangling feet.

"It's like a fucking Buddhist parable or something," said Tom. "About enjoying life's small pleasures in the midst of despair and uncertainty and all that."

"I've been dizzy and nauseous enough as it is, thanks," said Jordan.

Isaiah sat down on the ground and put his face in his hands.

"Wheeee," said Tom.

Jordan stopped the tire swing's gentle swaying and leaned back to reach into his pocket. He took out the vial of Milk and held it up. The light was dim and flickering here so he couldn't be sure, but it didn't look like there was very much left.

"Oh good," said Isaiah, looking up at him through splayed fingers. "The person who's hearing voices needs more drugs. But that's good, right? Because he wouldn't be able to tell us where we're going if it weren't for the voices."

"I haven't heard any better ideas," said Jordan. He unscrewed the eyedropper and put a drop on his tongue.

"Come on, man," said Tom. "Some of us are getting high on life over here. You should try it sometime."

Jordan jumped down awkwardly from the tire swing. He knelt down by Isaiah's backpack and rummaged around in the backpack for a sandwich, dropping the vial of Milk inside. He stopped rummaging and looked up.

"They're coming," he said.

Isaiah went pale.

"Are you fucking serious?" said Tom.

"We need to start running," said Jordan. "Right now."

Isaiah didn't move.

Tom jumped off the merry-go-round. He grabbed his backpack and slung it over his shoulder. He grabbed Isaiah by the arm. "Goddamn it," he said. "Which way?"

"That way," Jordan pointed down a dimly lit tunnel of twisting metal bars.

Tom started running, dragging Isaiah after him.

Jordan stood for a moment, staring into the metal canopy behind them, looking for movement. Nothing was moving. Or everything was. He felt dread build all around him like a cloud, thickening the air.

A high-pitched, inhuman shriek stabbed through it all like a needle.

It sounded like:

"EENEENEENEENEENEENEENEENEE"

Jordan turned and ran.

His small feet pounded on the rubber-padded ground. He didn't seem to be getting anywhere. He could see Tom and Isaiah up ahead, running into the tunnel. Tom yelled something but he couldn't make it out.

He tried to focus on driving his child-sized legs faster and faster.

"The path is going to branch," said the Olm. "Take

the left branch."

"Go left!" yelled Jordan. He was struggling to breathe. Something caught his sleeve, a sharp piece of metal protruding from the wall of the tunnel. It tore his shirt and he spun and fell. As he got up he glanced over his shoulder just in time to see a black shape darken the tunnel entrance. He dragged himself up and ran.

The shriek was deafening this time. He clapped his hands over his ears. His heart was pounding and his chest burned. He gasped for air.

"Your friends are almost out," said the Olm. "They need to climb the chairs to the door."

Jordan tried to yell, but he couldn't fill his lungs. Tom and Isaiah had disappeared around the corner in front of him.

Jordan could feel himself getting light headed. The tunnel branched in front of him. He veered left and something grabbed his ankle. He fell.

His head hit the rubbery ground and bounced and something, some hooting, flailing mass was on top of him. A plush tendril lashed around his neck and began to squeeze. He swung wildly, kicking and punching, and tendrils lashed around his arms and legs. He managed one choked scream before his windpipe pinched shut. The pressure in his head was unbearable.

His head flopped back and overhead he saw a red plush creature scampering along the ceiling of the tunnel. It glanced down at him with giggling googly eyes.

"EENEENEE!" it shrieked.

Jordan watched it reach the tunnel branch. He saw it turn left.

The world was getting quiet and narrow. He could feel it slipping away.

Something soft nuzzled up against his head.

"Oonoonoonoo," it said. Something clamped down hard on his nose and tore it off his face. He barely felt it. "Oonoonoonoo…"

He blacked out and died.

***

"This is bullshit!" said Tom.

The tunnel had opened abruptly into a clearing and a mountain of multicolored plastic chairs, piled haphazardly on top of each other.

"Trap," said Isaiah, gasping for air.

They heard Jordan scream behind them.

"Fuck it," said Tom. "Start climbing."

They scrambled up onto the pile. Chairs shifted and slid under their weight as they climbed.

"EENEENEE!"

"Trap," said Isaiah. He was crying now.

"Come on, fucker, climb!"

Above, at the top of the pile of chairs, there was a large wooden door.

There was a clatter of chairs below them.

Tom grabbed Isaiah's hand and pulled him up.

"Keep going," Tom said.

Tom stood, balancing himself on a chair as Isaiah climbed past him. Tom wrestled a chair out of the pile and held it over his head. About twenty feet below, a bright red muppet with foot-long tentacle fingers was flailing its way up the pile. It stared up at him with plastic googly eyes that wobbled as it climbed.

"Eeneenee!" it said.

Tom threw the chair downwards, striking the creature in the face. It reared back, wriggling its tendril fingers in the air.

"EENEENEE!"

"Ha ha! That's right, fucker!" yelled Tom.

Tom struggled to dislodge another chair.

"Tom!" called Isaiah from above.

The chair wouldn't budge. The red muppet lunged forward, bounding up the chair pile. Chairs toppled and slid under it. It fell back, regained its footing and lunged again.

Tom slung the backpack off his shoulder and held it with both hands, swinging it back and forth.

"Cocksucking motherfucking piece of fucking shit cocksucking…" he said.

The creature lunged forward again, wrapping a tendril finger around a chair and pulling itself forward.

"tittyfucking asshole mother fucker piece of shit cumguzzling son of a bitch!" said Tom.

The creature hurled itself at him and he swung the backpack, catching it in mid-air. As the backpack hit its muppet head and bounced it back like a tennis ball, Tom lost his grip on the strap. A red tendril whipped past his face and the muppet tumbled backwards down the pile in a cascade of falling chairs, tangled up in the straps of Tom's backpack.

"EENEENEENEENEEEEE!" it shrieked.

Tom let out a wordless triumphant yell.

"Tom!" Isaiah was yelling down at him. "Hurry!"

Tom scrambled up the pile. He could feel the chairs giving out under him. The whole pile was coming down. He slipped and hit his face on a chair and Isaiah grabbed his arm and dragged him up.

They toppled through the open door onto smooth tile. The clattering of chairs rose to a cacophony as the pile came down behind them. Isaiah struggled to his feet and slammed the door shut and the sound ended abruptly. He grabbed the deadbolt with shaking fingers and locked it.

"Yeah!" yelled Tom. "Fuck yeah!"

His voice echoed back at him.

Isaiah slid to the floor and buried his face in his hands.

***

"Ha! Yeah, that was pretty cool, I guess," said the Reverend Timmy. "I liked the part where that one kid got his nose ripped off. Like, 'got your nose!' Haha! Do we have any more coke? Can someone bring me some more coke?"

Part 4

The first sensation was pain. Jordan was prepared for that, but he wasn't prepared for the stench.

He came back to life gagging and retching. He rolled over and felt the ground shift and slide under him. He felt wet and sticky all over.

He opened his eyes and stared down at his naked body, stained dark red and realized he was lying on a pile of meat and organs and bones.

The dry heaves intensified, forcing shut his eyes and doubling him into a tight ball. Every breath brought another wave of stench. It was so thick he could taste it, rotting meat and the metallic tang of blood. He wondered if the gagging would ever stop.

He struggled to his feet and slipped, falling backwards into the pile and sliding downhill. Something sharp jabbed him in the back, probably a bone. White jellyfish swarmed around him in a cloud, disturbed by his movements. They floated haphazardly around his head, colliding with his face. He waved them away as he tried to stand again and made it a few steps before lodging his foot in a ribcage. He slid and tumbled down the hill of gore until he finally landed on the solid rubber ground of the New Equipment.

Jellyfish were landing on him, tasting the blood that covered his body with their tiny tendrils. He brushed them off, but they kept coming. He crawled away from the meat pile, leaving bloody streaks and handprints as he went. He rubbed at his body, trying to clean off the chunks of gore and clotted blood.

His skin had a strange texture now. It was a mosaic of flesh scraps held together with a mortar of dried Milk. It felt rubbery and inflexible.

"I bet you think this is pretty funny, don't you?" he said.

There was no answer.

Jordan, the meat pile, and the jellyfish were at the bottom of a wide and deep cylindrical pit. It was made of a tangle of brightly colored metal bars and lit by hanging lamps and protruding light poles. The meat pile was situated at one edge of the pit. The wall above it was splattered with blood and meat bits. He crawled across the floor, over to the monkey bar wall at the opposite side of the pit, gasping for air and swatting at jellyfish. They had mostly given up on him and returned to the pile.

Jordan sat with his back against the metal bars of the wall and looked up at the opening of the pit high above. The bars were uncomfortable but sensation was dulled throughout his body. Only the flesh patches could feel and each patch was insulated within the fine webbing of numb solid Milk.

He didn't realize he was dozing off until the sound of a distant scream startled him awake. He sat up, heart racing. For a few drowsy moments he wondered if his heart was as much of a glued together jigsaw puzzle as the rest of him. He figured it probably was.

There was another scream. Jordan shook his head to clear it. He stood up. The blood on his skin had mostly dried. It was brownish red and stuck to everything he touched. From above, somewhere in the distance, he could hear the familiar shrieking and hooting of the muppets.

Jordan paced in tight circles.

"You want me to get out of here right?" said Jordan. "I need to get out of here if I'm going to get to the top like you want me to."

There was no answer.

"Come on, asshole, what's my next move?" he said.

The shrieking and hooting was getting louder.

After a few moment's thought, Jordan took a deep breath and walked back to the meat pile and started rooting through the squishy mess. The bones were all child-sized, but he managed to find a reasonably sturdy femur and wrestle it out from the viscera.

He ripped the dangling tendons from the bone and held it in both hands like a baseball bat. He took a couple of practice swings with it. It made a satisfying swish in the air, but it didn't have as much heft as he would like.

They were close now. Almost to the edge of the pit. He took his femur and started looking for a place to hide.

There was no place to hide.

"Eeeneenee!"

He looked up and froze. A red muppet head poked out over the edge of the pit above. It twitched and shuttered and regurgitated a spray of chunky reddish-black liquid. The discharge of separated child parts took a few seconds to fall the distance of the pit. When it hit, a mass of white jellyfish exploded from the pile, swarming up around Jordan in a frantic cloud. Bodily fluids and tissues rained down on the pile in front of Jordan with a wet splattering sound punctuated by the occasional thump of landing bone.

The blue muppet stuck his head out next to the red one and unleashed its own spray of human byproducts.

Jordan stood perfectly still. Jellyfish collided with his face and fluttered past his ears.

A skull hit the top of the meat pile and tumbled down the slope, off the pile, and past Jordan's foot, rolling on the rubber floor and clattering into the metal tangle of the wall.

And the twin fountains of gore continued.

After what felt like a very long time, the red muppet choked out its last bit of vomit and withdrew. The blue one continued for a few more seconds, then stopped. It sat at the top of the pit, rocking back and forth, then stopped. It coughed and choked out a final skull.

"Oonoonoonoonoo," it said.

It turned away from the pit's edge and disappeared from view.

The jellyfish slowly began to settle. Jordan brushed them off and waved the bone around his head to shoo them.

***

Jordan paced around the bottom of the pit, test-swinging his femur.

"Seriously?" he said.

There was no response.

"Well fuck you too," he said.

Still no response.

Jordan started to sigh but the deep breath in made him gag.

"Fuck," he said. "Well I'm guessing the first step is to get out of this pit, so… I guess I'll start with that."

He circled around the pit until he found a spot that looked like a good place to start climbing. After some consideration, he dropped the femur on the ground. He was naked and he needed two hands to climb and he wasn't about to try holding the thing in his teeth.

While the pit wall was basically jungle gym material, it was not made for easy climbing. Bits of metal interwove in a chaotic tangle and sharp spikes protruded at random. The plastic-like dried Milk that made up a good percentage of Jordan's skin had the benefit of being numb, but it was slipperier and not as flexible as normal skin. It was difficult to maintain a grip. It wasn't long before his forearms burned and his grip began to feel weak. He wrapped his arms around the bars in front of him and hugged them against his chest to hold himself up as he rested. He looked down. The ground was far enough away to give him vertigo but still too close to feel like much of an accomplishment. He couldn't have been more than a third of the way up. Maybe not even a fourth. Jordan pressed his forehead against the bars and waited for the burning in his arms to lessen. Then he started climbing again.

***

"We can't just leave it locked like this," said Tom.

"We have to," said Isaiah.

"But we can't though," said Tom.

They were sitting on the checkered tile next to the door. They had been sitting there for quite a while. They were in what looked like a hallway from a fairly upscale house. It was very long and lined with doors and a series of identical potted plants sitting on identical small tables. Every surface looked polished and new.

"Do you really think he's going to make it?" said Isaiah.

"I don't see why not. What's the worst that could happen? He already died and came back once."

Isaiah rolled his eyes. "The worst that could happen," he said, "is that we leave this door open and those... things follow us in here and choke us to death and rip our skin off while we sleep."

"Those fucking muppets probably can't even turn door knobs."

"How do you know?"

"So we'll wait here until he gets here," said Tom.

"And how long is that going to take?"

"As long as it takes."

"And when we run out of food and water?" said Isaiah.

Tom sighed. "Well," he said. "Ok, I'll give you half the food and I'll take half the food and you can go do whatever the fuck it is you want to do and I'll wait here and we'll just see how that works out for each of us, how about that?"

"It would be safer if we stayed together," said Isaiah.

"Oh really? Then by that logic wouldn't it be even safer if all three of us stayed together? Isn't that how that works?"

They sat in silence for a moment. They had heard nothing through the door since the initial shrieking and clattering of chairs that had marked their entry.

"Well," said Isaiah. "I guess I'll go look around a little. Stay here. Don't leave without me."

"I won't," said Tom. "Leaving people behind isn't a thing that I do, in case you hadn't noticed."

Isaiah stood up and started walking down the hallway. It was absurdly long, but he could see the end in the distance. He walked down the rows of identical doors. He chose one at random and opened it. It opened into a spacious stairway landing with marble floors. He stepped into the space. Light was shining in through a translucent window above the door behind him. In front of him, the left flight of stairs went up and the right went down. He walked to the carved ironwood railing and peered over the edge. The stairs spiraled upwards and downwards as far as he could see.

He went back through the door and closed it behind him and tried the next door. It opened into a tiny bathroom with a sink and a toilet. The walls were covered in cheap flowery wallpaper and the floor was yellow linoleum. Isaiah tried the sink's cold water knob. Clear water poured into the basin. He cupped his hand and tasted a handful of water. It tasted clean. Opposite the sink there was a narrow white plasterboard door. Isaiah opened it to reveal an upwards staircase, this one narrow and steep and made of plywood. It smelled of sawdust. Isaiah closed the door and went back to the hallway.

"Well," he called to Tom, "I have a little bit of good news. I found some water." His voice reverberated in the hall. "I can fill up our canteen."

"Cool," said Tom. He didn't move.

Isaiah stared at him for a moment then walked back towards him. He knelt down next to Tom and opened the backpack.

"What's the bad news?" said Tom.

"I didn't say there was any," said Isaiah.

"The bad news is that it's just another fucking maze, isn't it?" said Tom.

Isaiah rummaged through the backpack until he found the canteen.

He took the canteen into the bathroom and filled it and brought it back to Tom. Then he walked back down the hall and tried another door. It opened into another hallway, this one with brown carpet and off-white plaster walls. It was long and dim and lined with doors.

***

"EENEENEE!"

Jordan flinched and nearly lost his grip. He twisted around, trying to find the source of the sound. There they were, both of them, on the opposite side of the pit, scurrying towards him around the rim.

Jordan froze. He looked up and then down, and immediately regretted looking down. They were coming too fast. He felt dizzy.

Eenee shrieked again, the sound stabbing Jordan's eardrums like a thorn.

Jordan took a deep breath and let it out slowly. "Fuck it," he said.

He stopped climbing and waited, watching the blue and red demon puppets crawl sideways and down on their fingers. Closer and closer. Jordan loosened his grip on the bars and leaned slightly backwards, struggling to ignore the terrified part of his brain. Eeenee was in the lead, flailing and wriggling over the bars, its shrieks increasing in volume and enthusiasm.

It pounced and dropped like a furry red meteor, screaming down at him, tendril fingers spread wide. Jordan let go of the bars and brought his arms up to meet it. With the sting of impact, Jordan jumped backwards off the wall and they were falling. He fought twist in the air to somehow get on top but he was wrapped in red felt tentacle fingers in an instant, barely able to move.

Jordan's last thought before he hit the ground was about how much he hated falling. He hit the ground and his head bounced off the rubber-coated plastic and he blacked out.

***

He was conscious a few seconds later. The wind was knocked out of him and he had a massive headache, but his body and bones seemed to be intact. Eenee was on top of him, choking him and biting at his face. Or trying. The muppet mouth that could normally peel children like grapes was bouncing off Jordan's rubbery Milk-infused skin. His neck flesh was too stiff for Eenee to squeeze shut his windpipe.

As his breath came back, Jordan found himself laughing.

Eenee was growing increasingly frustrated, shaking Jordan and yanking impotently at his arms, legs and neck. Jordan tried to punch at it but couldn't free his arms. He was simultaneously invulnerable and helpless. The blue one was trying to bite him now too.

"Oonoonoo?" it said.

"Eeneenee!" said Eenee.

With one last frustrated shriek, it heaved Jordan off the ground and threw him. He hit and rolled. He pushed himself up onto his hands and knees and Eenee lunged at him again, mouth gaping. Jordan got his hand up in front of his face, catching the muppet's head. It thrashed and chewed at his fingers as he pushed it away. Oonoo rushed in and tackled his legs, dragging him to the ground and biting at his calves. Jordan pushed his palm up into the roof of Eenee's mouth, forcing its head backwards as it tried again to choke him. He pushed his fingers up over the top of its head until he found the smooth hard lump of its plastic googly eye and grabbed it and yanked it. Eenee's shrieks turned from anger to pain. Its tendrils released and it struggled to push him away. Jordan clutched the eye and yanked it again and again until it tore free. Eenee leapt off him, shrieking and flailing on the ground, a thread dangling from its empty eye circle.

Oonoo scrambled up the length of Jordan's body and Jordan brought down a hammer fist on its squishy muppet head, Eenee's eye still clutched in his palm. Oonoo pulled back and struck like a snake, biting down on Jordan's clenched fist. It clampeed down and chewed and ground its hard, toothless jaws on the hand, unable to break through the rubbery skin or crack the Milk-hardened bone. Jordan leaned forward and grabbed Oonoo's head with his other hand. He held it and forced his fist into its mouth and down its throat. It thrashed and struggled as he forced his arm in past the elbow. He let go of the eye and grabbed on to the inside of Oonoo's plush stomach and grabbed its upper jaw with his other hand and pulled. He felt the fabric tear as he wrenched the muppet's stuffing up through its esophagus and out through its mouth.

"Eeneeneeeeee!" Eenee wailed behind him.

Jordan threw Oonoo's twitching inside-out body to the side and climbed to his feet.

"That's right!" he said. "That's fucking right! You fucking muppets!"

He turned to Eenee. It stared up at him with its remaining googly eye, cowering.

"Doesn't feel good does it?" he said. He took a step towards it. "And this isn't going to feel good either you evil fucking—"

Eenee shrieked and ran. Jordan chased after it. The red muppet hit the wall and squeezed its body into a space between the interlocking metal bars, compressing its body and wriggling its way inside. Jordan caught up just as it struggled to pull its back leg inside and snagged it by one of its tentacle toes and pulled.

"Eeneenee!"

It pulled forward. Jordan put a foot up against the wall to brace himself and pulled as hard as he could until the toe ripped off in a puff of stuffing and he tumbled backwards onto the ground, laughing and clutching the toe to his chest.

"EENEENEENEEEE!" the sound receded into the metal foliage of the pit wall.

Jordan jumped to his feet and threw the toe to the side.

"That's right! That's fucking right!"

He walked back to Oonoo's body, a no longer twitching pile of stuffing and fabric. He kicked it. No signs of life. He knelt down and started tearing off the stuffing and ripping at its seams.

"Fucking muppet piece of shit," he said.

Jordan fashioned himself a loincloth from Oonoo's skin and got back to climbing.

***

By the time he reached the top of the pit, Jordan was exhausted. He dragged himself over the edge and crawled across the hard rubber ground for a few feet before stopping. He rolled onto his back, breathing hard. The thirst had come on gradually, but now it was overwhelming. His mouth was dry, his head ached and deep in his stomach he could feel a desperate need for water.

"So this is it, huh?" he said, staring up into the tangle of the New Equipment. "You're just not going to talk to me now."

There was no answer. Two white jellyfish pulsated through the air past him, headed for the pit. Gradually, his breathing slowed, but the thirst was constant. He rolled over and pushed himself up onto his hands and knees and stood up, adjusting his muppet loincloth. The pit was in the center of a large circular clearing. Passageways radiated off in all directions. He counted twelve total.

"I'm getting really fucking sick of this scenery," said Jordan.

He paced around the clearing. The passageways all looked the same, just tunnels of colorful tangled metal.

"Come on man!" he said. "You want me to get to the top of this thing, right? Tell me which way to go! That's what you want, right? I thought you were the impatient one here. You stepped in because it was taking too long. You're the one who wouldn't shut the hell up. And now you're just going to go quiet? Just to fuck with me?"

The Equipment was utterly silent without even the hiss of a breeze.

"Just tell me what to do and I'll do it!" said Jordan.

He circled the clearing, peering down each passageway. No landmarks, nothing at all familiar. He had no idea how far he'd traveled in pieces in the muppets's stomachs, no idea where Tom and Isaiah were. They could both be dead, for all he knew.

Jordan stopped and sat down cross-legged on the ground. He put his head in his hands.

"Just tell me what to do," he said.

"EEE!"

The shriek startled him upright, sending a cold shock down his spine. There was a flurry of red motion to his left.

He jumped to his feet. Eenee was scampering sideways along the wall of the clearing. It stopped at the edge of the nearest passageway just a few yards away and looked up at him with its one eye, the black pupil wobbling.

"Eeneenee!" said Eenee.

In an instant, Jordan's fear turned to sick, burning hate.

"You little fuck," he said. "Do you think I'm scared of you? Don't you understand I'm fucking invincible?"

"Eenee!" said Eenee.

Jordan lunged forward and Eenee darted around the

edge of the passageway and scurried away. Jordan sprinted after it, bare feet hammering the hard rubber ground.

"I'm going to rip," said Jordan, between panting breaths, "your fucking guts out."

Eenee darted around a corner and Jordan followed, legs and lungs burning, head throbbing. Losing an eye and a toe had done nothing to slow the fucker down. It turned abruptly down a right-hand side corridor. Jordan slid trying to make the turn and bounced off the wall and kept running. He could feel himself starting to slow. He could see Eenee getting farther and farther away. Eenee rounded another corner up ahead. Jordan focused his anger and pushed himself forward, coming around the corner just in time to see Eenee scramble into a circular blue opening in the wall, about three feet in diameter and three feet off the ground. Jordan cleared the space and dove head first into the blue plastic tube.

He slid a few feet on the slick plastic and started dragging himself forward on his forearms and pushing off with his feet in a military-style crawl. Eeneenee had disappeared around a bend in the tube up ahead.

Jordan yelled a ragged wordless yell that reverberated back at him in the tube. Everything was tinted blue from light shining through the partially translucent walls of the tube. He rounded the bend and fell forward. He felt something wet on his arms and suddenly he was sliding down faster and faster. He tried to brace himself against the walls but everything was slick and slimy with grease. The downward tilt of the tube was increasing rapidly and he slid faster and faster down the slide, flailing, unable to get a grip on anything.

The tube slide got darker as he fell until he was hurtling forward in pitch blackness, his only points of reference being the feel of the wind on his face and the slippery sliding of the plastic on his skin and suddenly the plastic was gone and he was flying through the air.

For an instant he was suspended in pure rushing void, tumbling head over heels, and just as he was taking a breath to scream he hit the wall of spikes. A dozen sharpened rebar poles punctured his body at once, driving through the skin of his back and through muscle and organs and out through the skin of his front. For a fraction of a second there was no pain. Then it crashed down in a wave, all at once. And then there was a high pitched ringing in his ears and the pain began to fade as everything faded into shock and from somewhere up above he heard Eenee's high-pitched cries of joy and then the ringing swallowed everything and there was nothing.

***

"Sir?"

The Reverend Timmy lifted up his head. It felt much too heavy. His eyelids felt heavier. He was sitting in an armchair, slumped forward with his head in his hands.

"Must be nodding," he muttered.

"I'm sorry to bother you, sir, but you wanted to be informed if anything interesting happened in the New Equipment." He could make out the blurred image of a dark-haired woman in a tuxedo talking to him. He shook his head to clear it.

"Yeah, I guess I did say that," he said. His voice was low and gravelly.

"Would you like me to bring a monitor for you?"

Timmy fell back in his chair, waving his hand dismissively. "Nah, it's all good," he said. "Just make like… a highlight reel or something. I'll watch it later."

"Certainly," said the woman. "Can I get you anything else?"

"Uhhh," said Timmy. He shook his head to clear it. He looked around the room. There were a number of greasy bearded men passed out on various pieces of furniture and the floor. "Oh right. I guess make sure that none of these guys are dead. And uh… ask them if they need anything."

"Of course," said the woman.

"Do you know why all these hobos are in here?" said Timmy.

"I assume," said the woman in the tuxedo, "that it's because the Reverend's kindness and generosity is boundless."

"Damn right," said Timmy. "Charitable as fuck. Do you know how… charity is its own reward? That's what I'm doing, I'm rewarding myself by rewarding them. Because I'm a good person."

The woman smiled at him. "I'm glad to see you happy," she said.

"I fed them and bathed them, and gave them food and drink," said Timmy. "Or wait, I guess I didn't bathe them. See if anyone of them wants a bath. Also, make sure they aren't dead. I gave them a lot of heroin too. I want them to feel pleasure like I feel pleasure."

"Um," said a different woman in a tuxedo, this one nervous-looking. She must be new. Timmy considered tormenting her a little and then remembered his newly

170

exalted level of character, as demonstrated by this act of generosity. "This one... he's breathing, but not very well? And his pulse is weak? And I think he maybe threw up a little?"

"Which one?" said Timmy. "The one you're touching? Ok."

He concentrated. The circle on his forehead tingled and the homeless man gasped and started coughing. The nervous tuxedo woman jumped back, startled.

"Fix his lungs too so they don't do that," Timmy muttered. The man stopped coughing and started taking deep, even breaths.

"Holy hell," the man said.

"You ok there, buddy?" said Timmy. "You had a little too much of the good stuff, is all. It's all good now. I fixed you up. Because when you hang with the Reverend it's all pleasure and no bad consequences. Nothing bad happens in my fucking house, I don't allow it."

The homeless man was glancing around the room. He stared at the nervous tuxedo woman, confused. She smiled at him, nervously.

"You, uh," said Timmy. "You want a bath? I realize I didn't do the bathing part. Huh? You want a bath? How about if one of these nice ladies gives you a bath, you'd like that I bet, huh? Yeah you would. New girl, take my guest into one of my finest bathrooms and give him a good scrubbing. No, I mean, give him a nice leisurely, luxurious sort of bath, is what I mean."

"Would you like us to bring in some, uh, prostitutes as well?" said the dark-haired woman.

"Sure," said Timmy. "Yeah, that's a good idea.

Not my kind though, the normal kind. Or whatever they want. Give the men what they want, that's what I'm here for! Figure out what they want and give it to them."

The nervous woman reached for the homeless man's arm and he jerked back away from her. "This isn't one of those things is it?" he said. "One of those like Satanic blood rituals you rich folks do?"

Timmy laughed. "Now why would you think something like that?"

"It just seems like the only reason a rich person brings someone like me into someplace like this is for some weird occult shit, you know what I'm saying? You think someone like me doesn't have family or anyone looking out for him so we're like… easy targets or whatever."

Timmy laughed again. "My good sir," he said. "Have you so little faith in your fellow man? Is it so hard to believe that I want to make you happy because it makes me happy?"

"And why do you, a young child, have all this stuff, and heroin, and woman butlers? It don't make sense," said the homeless man. He was shifting nervously in his seat, running his hands through his hair and rubbing his beard. "I think I want to get out of here."

"Seriously?" said Timmy. "I just brought you back to life. I brought you back to life with my fucking mind. Don't you understand the kind of utter fucking jackpot you've stumbled into? With my fucking mind, bro!"

"Yeah I definitely want to get out of here," said the homeless man. He stood up and started backing towards the door, eying the women in tuxedos like they were snakes.

Timmy's eyes narrowed. He took a long, deep breath. "Fine," he said. He gestured towards the door. "The gentleman wants to leave. So please show him the way out, please. Thank you."

"Right this way," said the dark-haired woman.

The homeless man shuffled towards the door staring at Timmy.

"I only want people here who want to be here," said Timmy. He leaned forward abruptly, stabbing at the air with his finger. "This is fucking charity over here! I'm helping you out. And if you don't want the help, that's fine. Leave. I don't need ungrateful pieces of shit in my house. I don't want to hang out with ungrateful pieces of shit. I want to hang out with my fucking friends. So if you don't want to be my fucking friend then please, get the fuck out of my house you worthless fuck!"

The homeless man sprinted for the door. The nervous woman froze, eyes wide in confusion. The dark-haired woman speed-walked after him into the hallway saying "Sir! Sir, there is no reason to be alarmed."

"I brought you back to life with my fucking mind and I can kill you again too!" yelled Timmy. "With my fucking mind!"

He fell back into his easy chair, panting.

Most of the homeless men were awake now, either groggily lifting their heads or staring at Timmy in horror.

"This is what I get for being fucking nice," said Timmy. "Fucking ungrateful piece of shit." He looked up at the men. "You guys probably want to leave to, right? Because I so fucking evil for trying to do nice things."

A man in a tattered green trench coat glanced at the man next to him and back to Timmy. "Well," he said. "I don't know about everyone else but... Satanic blood ritual or no, I'm not turning down an opportunity to get my dick sucked for free."

Timmy laughed and slapped the arm of his armchair. "That's the spirit! Get this man his dick sucked! Dick-suckings for everyone! This is a goddamn party in here, fuck the haters, let's have some goddamn fun!"

More tuxedoed women were coming into the room, rounding up the heroin-addled homeless men and filing them out the door to guide them to the baths.

Timmy sat in his chair and watched, the homeless men shooting him occasional worried glances as they filed out the door.

Timmy gestured to the nervous tuxedo woman and she came to him.

"Get me a girl too," he said. "A mean one. Did we ever get a hold of the one... what's her name? The girl with the hair?"

The woman stared at him blankly.

Timmy sighed. "The girl? She had shiny hair, remember? Like, gold metallic hair? Didn't even really look slutty or anything. I liked her."

The nervous woman shook her head. "I... I don't think so. I can check... but I think that... I don't think so. But I can check."

"Nah, fuck it," said Timmy. "Just get someone. Any of the girls. Someone who can hurt me."

The nervous woman nodded and hurried to leave but the shuffling line of homeless men were blocking the door so she stood still and waited and played with her cufflinks.

***

"Ow!"

Tom jerked awake. He hadn't realized he was sleeping. He had dozed off sitting with his back to the doorframe.

"What? What is it?" he said.

Isaiah sucked in air through his teeth. "There's something sharp in the bag." Beads of blood were forming on his pointer finger and thumb. He squeezed his thumb and scraped at it with a fingernail, dislodging a tiny shard of glass. "Broken glass."

"Huh? Glass? What did we... oh shit!" Tom jumped up and ran over to Isaiah and the backpack. "Fuck, man, that must be Jordan's vial of milk, it must've broken. That shit is going to get all over everything, the food and everything, man!" He grabbed the backpack and pulled it over to him, kneeling down and reaching in to grab a sandwich. "Ohh right," he said. "Everything's in plastic bags. Thank fucking god. The last thing we need is to trip balls every time we take a bite of a sandwich. Unless... that stuff can't soak through plastic can it? Nah, that doesn't make sense. Right? I think we're good. Man, I bet it's still soaked into the backpack though. How are we going to clean this shit out? It's just one goddamn thing after another." He began unloading sandwiches from the bag, piling them next to it. "Do you think we can just use water?"

Isaiah was staring down at his bleeding fingers.

"Are you ok, man?" said Tom.

"The Milk is the jellyfish," said Isiah absently.

"Dude," said Tom. Something brushed his face and he flinched, waving at it with his hand. A tiny white jellyfish floated down just out of reach and pulsed back to float up and down at eyelevel, pulsing and dropping. Tom laughed. "Jesus," he said. He turned back to Isaiah. "Seriously, man, what the fuck is going on?"

Isaiah didn't answer.

"Oh fuck," said Tom. "You touched it didn't you? You got Milk all up in your cuts, didn't you? God damn it."

Tom reached over and touched Isaiah's arm. Isaiah inhaled sharply and looked up.

Tom flinched back. The jellyfish floated past his ear to settle on Isaiah's hand. It crawled up his thumb and dipped a tendril into the pearl of blood.

Isiah stared at it.

"Ok," said Tom. "Everything's ok. You're ok, you're just tripping. I'm guessing you aren't used to that but just be cool and in a few—"

"Quiet!" said Isiah. "I can hear him."

Tom raised an eyebrow. "Who?"

Isiah's lips moved silently. He stared at the jellyfish.

"The Olm," he said. "He's talking to me."

"Oh," said Tom. "This again."

A joyous smile bloomed on Isiah's face. "Yes," he said. "Yes!"

"What's his deal this time?" said Tom.

"He's going to guide us to the top," said Isiah. Tears were running down his cheeks. "He says it's not much farther now. He's going to take us there!"

"What about Jordan?" said Tom. "Ask him if he knows where Jordan is. Can he still talk to him?"

Isiah sat quietly. His smile faded. He nodded somberly. "Jordan isn't coming," he said.

"What?" said Tom. "Fuck that. Where is he?"

"The Olm says he's trapped," said Isaiah. "He says there's no way out. We must go on without him. We must follow the jellyfish to the top of the New Equipment."

Tom shook his head. "No, fuck that," he said. "I'm not going anywhere without Jordan."

Isiah looked at him with tear-blurred eyes. "Come with us," he said. "Come with me to salvation. He says when we reach the top, all will be saved. Jordan... the rest of them... even the dead." Isiah made a sound halfway between a sob and a laugh.

Jordan got up and started shoving sandwiches into his pockets. "I'm going to go back and find him," he said.

"All will be saved," said Isiah. "All will be set free."

"Yeah, that's cool and all," said Tom. "But I'm going back."

Tom reached into the backpack, careful to avoid any broken glass, and removed one of the canteens. He slung it around his neck.

"The Olm says you can do what you will," said Isiah.

"Oh good," said Tom. "I'm glad I have his holy permission."

He unlocked the door and opened it slowly, peering

around the edge. The colorful playground equipment was jarring in contrast to the long marble hallway but everything was still and quiet. Plastic chairs were scattered haphazardly around the clearing below the door.

He turned back to Isiah. "Well, good luck with the whole salvation thing," he said. He pushed the door fully open and lowered himself over the edge. His feet dangled in the empty air. He let go and dropped down into the pile of chairs with a crash.

Swearing and thrashing, he extricated himself from the tangle of chairs and chair legs and crawled out of the pile and headed out of the clearing, back down into the jungle gym.

Isiah sat and stared at the jellyfish on his hand, tears of joy running freely down his face.

After a few minutes, he nodded and climbed to his feet. The jellyfish left his finger and fluttered in the air near his face. Isiah held onto the doorframe with one hand and leaned out over the edge to grab the doorknob with the other hand and pulled the door shut, smearing the doorknob with blood in the process. The door latched with a hollow click. Isiah reached up to the deadbolt and locked it.

He picked up the backpack and slung it over his shoulder. The jellyfish did a slow loop de loop and pulsed off down the hallway and he followed.

***

"Sam!"

Samantha was crouched down, examining a delicate blue glass flower. She looked up.

"What is it?" she called back.

"Come and see!" Lilith was up ahead, out of sight through the trees of the glass forest.

Samantha stood up and stepped carefully around the flower. "Can't you just tell me what it is like a normal person?" she called.

"No no no, come look!" called Lilith.

The trees were beginning to thin. The consistency of the ground was changing. Colorful glass pebbles crunched against each other under Samantha's feet, but didn't shatter. Lilith appeared suddenly from around a tree and grabbed Samantha's hand, tugging her forward.

"Come onnn," she said.

"Jesus, I'm coming already! What is it that's so goddamn—"

They came out of the forest and Samantha stopped. Lilith let go of her hand and ran out ahead, laughing.

"Oh wow," said Samantha.

They were standing on beach. The colorful glass pebbles stretched out to a huge, glittering lake. Lilith ran out onto the surface of the lake and turned back to Samantha.

"All glass!" she said. She stomped demonstratively on the surface. "The water is made of glass, all the way down."

"Whoa," said Samantha.

At the lake's edge, the glass pebbles were submerged under a thin layer of clear glass that grew deeper and thicker as it extended from the shore. The glass of the lake was wavy and rippled, like sloshing water frozen in a single moment. Samantha stepped out cautiously onto the lake's surface.

"It's amazing, yes?" said Lilith.

"I've been seeing nothing but new amazing things for days now," said Samantha, "but yes."

"And look," Lilith pointed into the distance.

The blue wires stretched out above them over the lake in one long, taught bundle of wires hanging in the air, no longer supported by polls. And off in the distance a dark structure loomed. It was grey and circular with sloping edges, like the severed base of a cone. It was difficult to tell, but it looked very far away and very large.

"An island?" said Samantha.

"It must be the Computer!" said Lilith. "Look! If you see over to the side, there are more blue wires. They are far away and hard to see, but there are many of them. They go out away from it in all directions. It is the center of all the blue wires. The Computer!"

"Yeah," said Samantha. "That would make sense."

"We're almost there, come on!" said Lilith, tugging on Samantha's arm.

They walked over the lake quickly but carefully, occasionally holding on to each other for support. The glass was slippery and uneven.

"Fishes!" said Lilith, pointing. Frozen under the surface was a school of small glass fish, bright blue and orange. The glass lake was deep now, the bottom an unknown distance below them, disappearing into murky dark green.

Samantha looked up at the clear blue fake sky. Unobstructed by trees, the hugeness and uniformity of the dome was almost overwhelming. In the distance to their right, they could see a glass dolphin frozen in the crest of a small wave, its top half protruding from the water mid-jump.

As they walked, the grey building became incrementally larger. It seemed to be a solid concrete bunker, basically featureless. A large metal antenna extended from the top with large bundles of blue wires radiating out in all directions like the spokes of a wheel.

"There must be others," said Lilith. "There must be other cities. One for each. Right?"

"Yeah I think you're right," said Samantha. "That's crazy."

The bunker grew and grew until it loomed over them, though in the uniform glow of the sunless sky it cast no shadow. They walked and walked until finally colorful pebbled ground faded into view far below their feet, sloping up out of the green abyss and getting closer and closer to the surface as they walked. The bunker filled their view now. Samantha had to crane her neck back to see the top of it. Finally, the glass water broke in waves on another glass pebble beach. They stepped over a frozen crest and onto unsolid ground. The shifting pebbles under their feet was a welcome relief after the rock-hard surface of the lake.

Samantha stopped walking and sat down. She let herself fall over backwards and lay on the beach, staring up at the bunker wall. The pebbles were smooth and comfortable.

"Sam Sam! What are you doing?" said Lilith.

"I'm tired," said Samantha. "My feet hurt."

"But we're here! We finally found it!"

"Yeah, and it doesn't look like it's going anywhere," said Samantha.

She picked up a handful of pebbles and held them

above her, letting them dribble out between her fingers onto her chest. Lilith's footsteps crunched up next to her. Lilith stood over her, arms crossed.

"You should try this," said Samantha. "It's fun."

"Samantha," said Lilith. "Get up."

"God, fine. You don't have to use the authority-figure voice."

Lilith reached down and took both of Samantha's hands, helping her to her feet. She stood up and brushed the pebbles off and they walked towards the bunker.

In the wall up ahead, there was a door.

***

There was no pain this time. His wounds had healed around the spikes and the spikes were evenly spaced throughout his body.

Jordan hung motionless in the darkness. He couldn't move. He had tried many times, first cautiously, then frantically. The spikes were metal rebar. Ribbed to bind with concrete, they had bonded to the Milk scabs of his wounds. He couldn't move anything but his fingers, toes and mouth.

The hunger and thirst were constant and unending. His breaths were quick and shallow, limited by the spikes through his lungs. The spike through his throat made it impossible to scream. The spike through his skull made it impossible to turn his head.

The panic came in waves. His body would tense, desperate to move, struggling for even an inch of progress. He would strain and struggle until his muscles failed from exhaustion. Then he would hang limp, crying in frustration. He would try to give up. He would tell himself there was nothing to be done, to just relax and accept it. His mind would wander and he could forget for a few seconds at a time where he was and what was happening and then all at once he'd remember that he was trapped forever and he couldn't die and the panic would crash down on him again in a wave.

He decided that his job was to control the panic. He focused on slowing his breath down, carefully monitoring the inhalation and the exhalation. But it always came back.

He decided to not control it, to just let it happen. He monitored the cycles of panic and despair and tried to think of it like the weather. Sometimes he could reach that mindset, detached and observing his body and then he would plunge back into it. He monitored the waves of attachment and detachment.

How long had it been so far, he wondered. Hours? Days? Minutes? It didn't matter. All time collapsed into the eternal present. Silence and darkness. The gentle tug of his bodyweight on the spikes. The wetness of the tears on his cheeks. Forever.

As time went on, his periods of struggle grew weaker and weaker. Exhaustion piled on exhaustion. His panicked thoughts would grow more and more confused. He would realize he was falling asleep, snap back awake, and repeat.

"It's a question possibilities," she said.

He could see her. She had red-orange hair and freckles and royal blue eyes.

"I'm dreaming, aren't I?" said Jordan.

"Yes, but don't think about it too much," she said.

They were lying in a bed. He could see the familiar unchanging light of the lower level filtering in through the window onto the blank white walls. It was all so clear.

"Don't think about it too much or you'll wake yourself up," she said.

He woke up with a gasp back in the darkness.

He observed another cycle of panic attacks and the slow descent of his thoughts into confusion and non sequiturs and he was asleep again.

"See?" she said.

"That's probably going to keep happing," said Jordan.

"Probably," she said. "But that's ok. Everything is ok, you see?"

"I keep trying to tell myself that," said Jordan.

"And it won't work and that's ok too," she said.

"I keep trying to tell myself that too," said Jordan.

She laughed. "Well yeah. I'm just you, I'm not going to tell you anything you haven't already told yourself."

"It's about possibilities," said Jordan.

"Exactly," she said. "There are none. So nothing you do matters."

"So why can't I stop caring about it?" said Jordan.

"It doesn't matter that you can't stop caring about it," she said. "It just is."

"I keep telling myself that," said Jordan.

"That doesn't matter either," she said. "And it's ok to keep doing it. Or not keep doing it. Everything is ok. See?"

"Yeah," said Jordan. "I know. But I still feel bad."

"It doesn't matter how you feel," she said. "Feeling bad is ok too."

"Except for the 'bad' part," said Jordan. "That's kind of the definition of 'bad.' It means 'not ok.'"

She shrugged. "Ok, so it's not ok. What are you going to do about it?"

"Nothing," said Jordan.

"Exactly."

"Probably keep waking up and falling asleep. Having panic attacks," he said. "Falling asleep. Waking up."

She smiled at him. He could see her smile so clearly. The stray strands of hair. The complex blue textures of the iris of her eye.

"See?" she said.

"I wish I weren't alone," said Jordan.

"That's ok too," she said.

He stared up at the ceiling. He could see the texture of the plaster. Sharp and clear.

"Can you touch me?" he said.

"If I do, you'll wake up again," she said.

"Try."

Her fingers were cold on his cheek and he woke up in the dark and realized he was crying again.

***

Isaiah followed the white jellyfish up a flight of old oak stairs. The steps were large for his child-sized gait. He pulled on the bannister for leverage. The walls were dark wooden paneling.

"I have so many questions," he said.

"All will be revealed in time," said the Olm in his head.

Isaiah stopped suddenly. "Actually," he said. "I only have one question, really. Why did my friends die?"

"The Lord works in mysterious ways," said the Olm.

"No!" Isaiah was startled by the sudden volume of his own voice. "That is not an acceptable answer."

There was silence. Isaiah stood on the stairway. The jellyfish flew in agitated circles over his head. His religious elation had collapsed all at once into a hard nugget of anger in his stomach. His fist was clenched.

"Listen," said the Olm. "I had nothing to do with that."

"Then who did?" said Isaiah. "Who was responsible?"

"You know the Good Reverend Timmy? Who you heard so many great things about but hardly ever saw?" said the Olm. "The Good Reverend is an asshole, OK? He's the one who filled this place with traps and monsters. Just so he could watch kids die on TV. Because he's a sadistic asshole. Understand?"

"No," said Isaiah. "I don't understand."

"I already told you," said the Olm. "When we get to the top, all will be saved, even the dead."

"And why should I trust you?" said Isaiah. "If he's such a bad person, why do you work for him?"

"I don't 'work' for that little fuck," said the Olm. "I work with him. Out of necessity. The only one I serve is God."

"God? Where was God when my friends were torn to pieces by those... things? Why did He let that happen? Why did He let Timmy claim to be working in

His name when it was all a trick?" said Isaiah. His voice shook as he spoke.

"You don't get it," said the Olm. "None of you do. God doesn't work like you think. He doesn't hear your prayers or hopes or dreams. He's too big for that. Do you understand how incredibly big He is and how incredibly small we are? We are nothing. We are tiny specks in his body, smaller than fleas, smaller than bacteria. Your life and the life of your friends mean nothing to him. You people are all the same. All you care about is yourselves and your worthless little lives. Do you know why Timmy does the horrible things he does? Because he's like you. Selfish. You people always have the best intentions in the world until you get a little power. I've seen it over and over. Every time. Just once, I'd like to see it go another way, but it never does. They get that dot on their forehead and no matter how nice they were before, how pure their original motives, once they know the truth and realize there are no consequences for them, it always goes the same way. Every single time.

"But I don't even care anymore," said the Olm. "What I'm doing is so much bigger than that. You people have your little dreams and goals and fantasies and you suffer and complain your whole lives. I'm done caring about that. I'm the only one who understands. I'm the only one who knows what must be done and I am going to do it. I don't care if it takes a thousand years. You people are all so busy hurting each other you don't realize that you're also hurting God. We are in God, but we are separate from him. And that separation hurts us, but more importantly it hurts Him. Forget

187

anything Timmy has done, forget your own little sins, your collective sin is far greater than that. You're hurting God. All of you. And I'm going to fix it. I'm going to stop this endless cycle. It seems endless, but I'm making progress. The cycles are accelerating, getting faster and shorter. It's only a matter of time. And like I said, I don't care if it takes a thousand years. I am going to fix what's broken between God and us. We will be reunited and there will be no more suffering, for us or for Him. And it's not just that.

"We are killing God, kid," said the Olm. "If I don't do this, we will kill him. And if you don't get to the top of this ridiculous fucking tower, you will be just as responsible for His death as anyone else. Is that what you're going to do? Stand by and do nothing while God dies all around us? Or are you going to help me save Him?"

Isaiah stood on the stairway. He looked back the way he'd come. He looked back up the stairs. At the top of the stairs, there was a large wooden door.

He started climbing again.

"I know you don't know what to believe any more," said the Olm. "But believe me when I tell you that this is the only way. Get to the top and God will send his angels down from Heaven to save us all and then we can be whole."

"I'm already climbing again," said Isaiah.

***

Lilith and Samantha approached the door. It was a plain gray metal door with a handle on it. It looked more like the door to a public school room than it did the entrance to a military-style bunker.

"So…" said Samantha. "Should we knock or…"

Lilith tried the handle. There was a click and the door swung open silently on well-oiled hinges. Inside was a brightly lit concrete corridor. Lilith and Samantha looked at each other. Lilith held the door and gestured for Samantha to go first. They walked into the bunker and Lilith shut the door gently behind them.

The lighting in the corridor seemed to come from everywhere and nowhere in particular. The ceiling was a tangled mess of metal pipes and blue wires, the walls and floor were featureless gray concrete. There was a low humming sound. Lilith touched the wall with her fingertips and felt a low tingling vibration.

They walked down the corridor until they came to a four-way intersection. Where the hallways met, a sign hung from the ceiling.

"What does it say?" said Samantha. The lettering was a language she didn't recognize.

Lilith stared up at the sign, chewing her lip. "Nursery that way," she said, pointing down the right hallway. "But it's not exactly 'Nursery'… I don't know how to say it. 'Person Garden?' I don't know." She pointed straight ahead. "This one says 'School' or… 'Learning?' 'Learning Room?'" She pointed to the left. "And that way it says 'Sleep Rooms' or 'Sleeping Rooms.'"

"I have no idea what to make of any of that," said Samantha.

"I don't know either," said Lilith.

"We're looking for a computer, right? None of them say 'computer?'"

Lilith shook her head.

"Which way should we go?" said Samantha.

Lilith's brow furrowed with concern. "I don't know," she said.

"Hmm," said Samantha. "Well, 'People Garden' sounds kind of horrifying. So I'm going to say no to that one. 'School' sounds kind of boring. So maybe let's try 'Sleep Rooms?'"

Lilith stared up at the sign, mouthing the words silently.

"Yeah?" said Samantha. "Maybe? Sleep rooms?"

"Ok," said Lilith. She didn't sound very sure of herself.

They turned to the left and started walking.

"The computer has to be in here somewhere," said Samantha. "I'm sure we'll find it. Maybe we can ask for directions. It seems like there's people here." Samantha stopped abruptly and grabbed Lilith's arm. Lilith stopped. "People," said Samantha, suddenly very nervous. "There are people in here."

Lilith looked preoccupied and confused. "Yes?" she said.

"We don't know anything about them," said Samantha. "What is this place anyway? It looks like a military bunker. We don't know anything about the people who live here, how do we know it's safe? How do we know they aren't assholes?"

"I don't know," said Lilith. "I don't know what to do. Should we leave again?"

"Well, I mean," said Samantha, "that would be kind of a huge let-down but…"

"Yeah," said Lilith.

"Since we walked all the way here, I mean," said

Samantha. "It's just so weird that there are people way out here in the middle of nowhere."

"Yeah," said Lilith.

They stood in the hallway. It was quiet except for the constant hum.

"Well," said Samantha. "You're sure that the Computer is here?"

"The blue wires always go to the computer," said Lilith.

"And you said the Computer is good, right? That it loves us?"

Lilith nodded.

"So then the people here should be good too, right?" said Samantha. "If they work with the computer? That would make sense, right?"

"I hope so," said Lilith. "I hope that's true."

Samantha shrugged. "Good enough for me," she said. "And I'm sure as hell not going to walk all the way back without at least doing a little investigating. I say we check it out."

"Ok," said Lilith.

"Come on! You've been so enthusiastic this whole time! You could at least act a little more excited to be here!"

Lilith smiled but her eyes looked worried. "I know," she said. "It's just… I don't understand. I don't know what this place is. It's all my responsibility. I brought you all the way out this far and now I'm afraid something bad will happen."

"Nothing bad is going to happen," said Samantha. "And if it does… well, whatever."

Lilith hugged her so abruptly she flinched.

"Don't die," said Lilith.

"Ok, ok, I won't!"

"Please don't die."

Samantha hugged her back awkwardly. "It's ok," she said. "I promise I won't die. Ok? Everything is going to be fine."

Lilith released the hug and turned away, wiping her eyes with the backs of her hands.

"You ok?" said Samantha.

"Yeah," said Lilith.

"Do you want another hug? I kind of fucked that one up. I can give you a better hug…"

Lilith laughed. "I'm ok," she said.

"You sure?"

"I probably scared you," said Lilith, "I'm sorry."

"No, no it was adorable. Unexpected, but adorable," said Samantha.

Lilith laughed again. She took a deep breath and let it out slowly. "Do you still want to see?"

"Let's do this!" said Samantha.

The corridor twisted and turned a couple times and then they rounded a corner and stopped. The hallway was lined with doors. Each door was metal, painted light blue with a circular window at eye level.

"Sleep Rooms?" said Samantha. "I guess we should be quiet," she whispered.

Lilith turned up her palms in a "your guess is as good as mine" motion.

Samantha gestured for Lilith to wait. She sidled up to one of the doors on their left and peeked in through the circular window.

"It's just a guy on a cot," whispered Samantha.

"Looks like he's sleeping. So that makes sense." She sidled up to the next door. "Whoa!" She whisper-yelled. "This is weird as fuck! It's like the exact same guy sleeping in here. He looks exactly the same."

Lilith cautiously moved towards the closest door to her right.

"Dude!" whispered-yelled Samantha. "It's the same guy sleeping in every room! This is super weird."

Lilith came up to the door. She peered in the window, cupping her hands around her eyes to block out the reflection.

Lilith gasped and stumbled backwards, covering her mouth with her hand.

"What?" said Samantha. "What is it?"

"Hello," said a calming masculine voice.

Samantha whirled around, fists raised.

A blue robot stood at the end of the hallway. It was vaguely humanoid with smooth blue plastic skin and a blank blue face.

"The fuck!" said Samantha.

"Don't be alarmed," said the robot. "I mean you no harm. Hello! And welcome."

"Why is it him?" cried Lilith. "How can it be him?"

***

"I'm dreaming again," said Jordan.

The redheaded girl smiled at him. "How do you know?" she said.

"Seems pretty obvious," said Jordan.

They were standing in a sandy wash next to a big white tree with no leaves.

"What if this place is real," said the girl, "and the

other place is the dream."

"I can tell this isn't real," said Jordan. "I wish I couldn't. But I can. I can always tell."

"At least you're coming here more often," said the girl. "And it seems like you're staying longer too."

"I think so," said Jordan. "I think it has something to do with being in the dark all the time. But I can't tell for sure. My sense of time is completely messed up. Every minute awake feels like eternity."

"It is eternity," said the girl.

"Thanks for reminding me," said Jordan.

He paced around the base of the tree. If he concentrated, he could make things clearer. He could add detail. The edges of the wash were lined with yellow grass and withered bushes.

"The one thing that never goes away is the thirst," said Jordan.

"I'm sorry," said the girl. She was leaning back against the tree, her arms folded in between her first and second pair of breasts.

"You're not real," said Jordan.

"Didn't Lilith give you a whole speech about that once?" said the girl. "About dreams and what's real?"

"Yeah," said Jordan. "I don't remember the specifics though."

"Me neither," said the girl.

"Why am I dreaming about you anyway?" said Jordan. "Why aren't I dreaming about her instead?"

The girl laughed. "That doesn't seem like a polite thing to ask," she said.

"Seriously though."

"Do you really want to see her?" said the girl.

Jordan felt a sinking in this stomach. "I don't know," he said.

"Do you think she'd ever forgive you?" said the girl. "Do you think you could even dream that she would?"

"I don't know," said Jordan. "Maybe not."

"So I guess you're happy it's me after all," said the girl. "You're welcome."

"I killed you, didn't I," said Jordan quietly.

The girl shrugged. "Not on purpose," said the girl.

"I didn't kill Lucas on purpose either," said Jordan. "But he's still dead."

"That was more on purpose than what happened to me," said the girl. "You just gave me some bad drugs, that's all. You didn't want me to die."

"I didn't want Lucas to die either," said Jordan.

"Really?" said the girl. "Do you remember how the Olm said the Milk works? I does what it's told to do. You told it to kill Lucas because you willed him dead."

Jordan stopped pacing. He sat down in the sand under the tree and put his head in his hands. The girl walked over to him and stood, looking down at him. She was wearing a thin blue dress that blew in the wind. Jordan couldn't feel the wind at all.

"And you?" said Jordan. "Why did you die?"

"The Milk was in me," said the girl. "I must have willed that too."

"Why would you do that?"

The girl shrugged. "Maybe I was just made that way," she said. "Wanting to."

"I wish I could change that," said Jordan.

"You can't," said the girl.

"I wish I could change everything."

She smiled sadly at him. "You can't. You can't change anything now. It's just this. Forever."

"I'm sorry," said Jordan. He was starting to cry.

"No one can hear you," she said and the world collapsed into blackness as Jordan woke from the dream.

"I'm sorry," he sobbed. "I'm sorry."

His body went limp.

"I'm sorry."

His eyes started to burn. There was a gush of liquid down his face and the salty taste of tears in his mouth changed to a different taste. The alkaline taste of Milk. His eyes had turned to Milk and poured down his cheeks.

Everything was burning now, all over his body. Everything felt wet. Liquid dribbled down on the spikes below him as his skin melted from his muscles. His mind was filling with a grey haze. He couldn't concentrate. All he could feel was an incredible emptiness at the center of his body.

As his muscles melted, his skeleton rattled on the spikes, dropping organs that turned to Milk as they fell.

As the last of him melted away, Jordan felt the familiar sensation of dying. His emptiness opened to all emptiness and he was free.

***

Isaiah followed the jellyfish up and up. He didn't say much to the Olm and the Olm didn't say much to him, other than to warn him of the occasional trap. Once, while walking down a hallway with dirty orange carpet and paisley wallpaper, he passed an open door. Inside was a bedroom. Lacey blue curtains were blowing in a perpetual breeze and a woman sat on the bed, with her back to the door. Her greying hair was tied up in a tight bun at the back of her head. When Isaiah saw her, he froze and his stomach froze.

"Don't go in there, for crying out loud," said the Olm. "You don't need me to tell you that's a bad idea, get away from that."

Isaiah turned and walked briskly away down the hall, the jellyfish fluttering a few yards ahead. He reached another staircase and climbed as quickly and quietly as possible. He glanced over his shoulder. The hallway was empty behind him.

"I'll be sure to give you a heads up if something is about to murder you from behind," said the Olm. "Don't you worry about that."

He walked through a kitchen with a yellow-checkered linoleum floor and a maze of cupboards and counters. He walked through a narrow corridor between two rows of identical white refrigerators. The staircases he climbed ranged from elegant marble to claustrophobic attic stairs that smelled of mildew and dust. He crawled along the top of a huge bookcase, pressing himself up against the wall on his right. To his left, the bookcase stretched down fifty feet or more. Across from it, about eight feet away was an equally tall set of metal shelves lined with rows of identical blank blue milk cartons.

He crawled out through an air duct into what looked like the waiting room of a doctor's office. The carpet was a rich royal blue. The walls were lined with blue padded chairs. Wooden coffee tables were strewn with magazines with pictures of teddy bears on them and no text.

"Getting close now," said the Olm.

The jellyfish floated against a glass door with a metal frame. Through the glass, there was nothing but sky and clouds.

Isaiah pushed open the door and a gust of fresh, cold air poured in. Isiah breathed in deeply. He hadn't realized how much he had missed the outside air. He stepped out onto a white-painted metal catwalk. The edges of the catwalk were covered with large chunks of cotton fluff like imitation clouds. Isaiah peered over the edge. Real clouds drifted below, and far below that was the distant ground. Vertigo set in and he quickly looked away.

"Is this it?" he said. "Am I at the top?"

"The top of the New Equipment, yes," said the Olm. "But you aren't done yet. You still need to go up to the next level."

"And the next level is paradise?" said Isaiah.

"Yep," said the Olm.

Isaiah's heart was racing. Up ahead, the catwalk led to a white-painted ladder that protruded twenty feet up into the sky and stopped abruptly. The jellyfish floated over to the ladder and fluttered around it in haphazard circles.

Isaiah walked down the catwalk to the ladder and started climbing. His palms were sweating and his hands shook as he tried not to think about how high up he was and how the thin rungs of the ladder were the only thing preventing him from falling down and down and bursting on the ground like a balloon of blood. He was approaching the top of the ladder.

"Do you see the rope?" said the Olm.

Isaiah reached the top. He squinted into the bright glowing blue of the sky dome. In the air in front of him was a small white rope, dangling from the dome.

"Yeah," he said.

"Pull on it," said the Olm.

He pulled on the rope and a hatch opened in the sky dome. It swung down to reveal a folded metal ladder. Isaiah unfolded the ladder, bracing its feet on the top rung of his current ladder. He climbed up the forty-five degree angle of the folding ladder up into the hatch. As he passed the rim of the hole in the sky, he reached out and touched the blue dome. It was cool to the touch and tingled slightly. The hatch opened into a small, dark cavern. The floor wasn't much more than a foot thick. In the small cavern there was another ladder that lead up to another metal catwalk that lead to an elevator. Isaiah climbed up to the platform and walked to the elevator door. He pulled open the metal gate door of the elevator with a rusty rattle and the shriek of poorly oiled hinges. The jellyfish drifted past his face into the elevator. He followed it in and closed the gate behind them.

"Pull that lever," said the Olm, "and brace yourself."

Isaiah pulled the level. The elevator lurched once, then started grinding upwards accelerating slowly at first, then faster and faster. Isaiah struggled to stay standing as the force of the acceleration increased. He felt like he weighed two or three times his normal weight. After what seemed like a very long time, the force finally let up as the elevator's speed leveled off. After what seemed like another very long time, Isiah began to feel lighter and lighter as the elevator began to slow. After another very long time, the elevator lurched to a stop and Isaiah stumbled, trying to adjust to his normal weight.

"You are very close now," said the Olm.

Isiah opened the elevator gate and stepped out into a cave. It was very dark, with a small space illuminated by the dim yellow light of the elevator. The jellyfish pulsed out in front of him, disappearing into the darkness, then gradually fading back into view. It began to glow brighter and brighter until it was a ball of white light that hurt to look at directly. The ball of light moved off into the cave, casting a pool of illuminated cave floor in a circular space around it. The walls and the ceiling were too far off to see, somewhere hidden in the blackness an indeterminate distance away. Isaiah hurried after the jellyfish, trying to keep his feet in the pool of light, looking down at his shoes scuffing on the bare rock of the ground.

He followed the jellyfish into a tunnel. The ceiling was lined with dead light bulbs in metal wire cages hanging from a central power line. The jellyfish was moving faster now, he had to quicken his pace to keep up.

"Almost there," said the Olm.

The tunnel ended at a ladder. Isaiah followed the jellyfish up the ladder, up through a hole a cement floor. They were in a small dusty room with brick walls. A pickax lay on the floor next to the hole. There was a row of metal shelves on one wall, lined with glass jars filled with an opaque liquid.

"Just up the stairs now," said the Olm.

The jellyfish flew up a flight of old, warped wooden stairs to an old wooden door. Isaiah followed, the wood creaking unstably under his feet.

"Open the door," said the Olm.

Isaiah grasped the worn metal knob and turned it. The latch came unstuck with a click and the door creaked open. The jellyfish darted out. Isaiah stepped through into another dark space. The jellyfish fluttered up, its light spilling over the ruins of a house, a skeletal frame of two-by-fours, a collapsed ceiling, a broken couch. The jellyfish flew up through the ribs of the ceiling and into the black open air.

"I don't understand," said Isaiah.

The jellyfish's light began to pulse. It began to emit a high-pitched whine.

"What is this place?" said Isaiah. "I don't understand."

He stood in the middle of the dilapidated living room. The light of the jellyfish strobed over surfaces of shattered wood and bricks. The high pitched whine was growing louder and louder.

"Answer me!" said Isaiah. "Where am I? What is this?"

There was no answer.

Isaiah stumbled through the living room to the frame of the front door out onto a concrete patio. In the dim pulsing light of the jellyfish he could barely make out the forms of steps leading down to the remnants of a street below, chunks of asphalt and dirt, and across the street, barely visible, more skeletal remains of houses and piles of rubble.

The high-pitched whine of the small jellyfish grated

on his ears and suddenly an incredibly loud and incredibly deep sound rang out from somewhere in the distance. He turned towards the sound. Off in the blackness, he could see a blurry ball of light. The deep sound rang out again. The ball of light was growing bigger and bigger. He could make out the silhouettes of backlit far-off buildings in it aura.

The light grew and the low sound got louder. The vague blur was beginning to take on a shape: a curved top and dangling tendrils. A glowing white jellyfish, large and distant, suspended in the air. As it got closer, it got bigger. The small jellyfish's whine amped up to a higher interval. The low sound was getting louder and clearer, a deep organic sounding groan.

Isaiah reached out at the approaching jellyfish. It seemed suspending in the air just in front of him, about the size a jellyfish should be, but he realized it was still far away. Much farther. It was growing faster now. The silhouettes of buildings were tiny in comparison. As it approached, another low rumbling joined the sound of the groan. The jellyfish towered over the ruined city. In its glow, Isaiah could see tiny buildings crumble in its wake. Its tendrils crackled with energy, bright white writhing flashes of lightning. The rumbling of thunder and collapsing buildings grew, but even that was dwarfed by the periodic swell of the groan. Isaiah clapped his hands over his ears. He could feel the sound in his chest. He craned his head back, staring up at it. The jellyfish spanned the horizon, the white folds of its body rippling like a storm front, massive tendrils hanging down over the city, lightning jumping from them to the walls of buildings and the empty shells of cars.

The groan was so loud now it shook everything. Bits of debris rained down from the frame of the house. The air vibrated in Isaiah's lungs, making it difficult to breathe. His body tingled as the air filled with static charge. His hair stood on end. The tendrils were massive tubes of white light, larger than skyscrapers. Everything was collapsing around him. Lightning struck nearby and the shockwave pushed him backwards. The tendrils were all around him now and the jellyfish filled the sky. Isaiah was screaming, but he couldn't even feel the vibration of his scream against the waves of sound that rocked his body. He screamed up into the massive rippling folds like a pure white aurora and in a blinding flash of lightning his body disintegrated into dust.

The jellyfish settled over the ruins of the house and began to sink. Its tendrils settled on the ground and the ground began to glow and melt. As the jellyfish settled to the ground, covering several city blocks with the house at its center, the ground became a pool of liquid rock. As the jellyfish sank down into the lava, the skyline of the broken city was dotted with more white lights. More jellyfish. Hundreds of them, heeding its call.

***

In his house, two levels below, the Olm sat up in his bathtub of Milk, gasping for air, milk pouring off his smooth pink head.

"Finally!" He said, rubbing his head with his tiny hands. "God, that took forever."

***

"In order to explain why that man is here," said the

203

robot, "And why there are so many of him, I will need to explain a lot of other things first."

They were in the Learning Room. Lilith and Samantha were seated in the middle of an auditorium. The chairs were padded and blue and the seats flipped up vertically if they were empty. Lilith was sitting silently, her arms wrapped around her middle. Samantha was sitting next to her. She kept glancing at Lilith, worried.

"What's wrong?" She had said, back by the Sleep Rooms. "Do you know this guy?"

"Yes," Lilith had said.

"How? Who is he?"

"A murderer," Lilith had said.

And then the robot had brought them here. It had been a long, awkward walk to auditorium.

"To be honest," said the robot, "I'm not entirely sure where to begin." It was standing at the front of the classroom next to a blank projector screen. It stroked its blue plastic chin thoughtfully.

Samantha glanced at Lilith. Lilith stared silently ahead.

"Where's the Computer anyway?" said Samantha. "Can we talk to it?"

"Unfortunately no," said the robot. "The Computer is not in one place. It is a vast network of software and hardware spread across this whole level. You could speak to one of its multiplicity of AI programs, derived from humanoid robots such as myself, but I am here to speak on its behalf. The most important thing is that the Computer loves you both very much."

"Yeah, we're aware of that part," said Samantha.

"I'm glad," said the robot. "Well how about this:

are you aware of the white liquid substance colloquially referred to as 'Milk?'"

"Yup," said Samantha. "It's a drug. I've done lots of it."

"Well, that is partially true," said the robot. "Milk can serve as a drug because Milk can serve as absolutely anything. The white liquid is the neutral, base form of what is called 'programmable matter.' It is matter that can alter its physical properties in every possible way known to the physical sciences. It is made up of pseudo-atomic structures that can generate protons, neutrons and electrons in any desired combination. It can be programmed to take any form."

The projector screen lit up with a rapid series of arbitrary gray objects on a pink background. Cooking utensils, cars, shoes, umbrellas, bicycles, toys, houses, plastic bags, spaceships...

"Humans invented programmable matter many years ago to fulfill their needs and desires. Many saw it as the ultimate logical conclusion of the practice of science. With this substance, humans could alter their environment at will. Humanity used this technology to spread out into space, gathering the energy from many, many stars until they had manufactured enough programmable matter to satisfy their every conceivable need. Programmable matter could be used to build cities, construct spaceships, as well as form any and all consumer products. Eventually the software available for programmable matter had become so advanced that elaborate fantasies worlds could be constructed for individual consumers. Even biological entities could be created from the substance, resulting in trees, animals, and ultimately pseudo-humans. Pseudo-humans were first used as slaves, then gradually became recognized as citizens in their own right. It was a very long and interesting process, but it is not really necessary information for answering your question."

Some images of protesters holding signs appeared on the projector screen. "People not P Zombies" one sign read. The images on the screen did not look like photos, but had the unreal, slightly uncanny quality of computer generated images.

"As humanity spread throughout their arm of the galaxy, the abundance of programmable matter began to outweigh the available natural resources. Real matter elements necessary for life, especially heavier atoms such as carbon, began to run out. As populations grew and food supplies dwindled, humans began to eat programmable matter food. Of course, the practice of eating programmable matter food would eventually replace all of the natural atoms in a human's body with programmable matter atoms, essentially rendering them pseudo-human after several years. People were well aware of this fact, but almost no one was upset by it. Humans and pseudo-humans had already been interbreeding for generations. There was practically no difference between the two subcategories in the mind of the average citizen. Eventually, there was no more normal matter food and there were no more normal matter humans left."

A diagram of the human digestive system appeared on the screen, followed by a diagram of the life-cycle of cells.

"Wait," said Samantha. "Are you saying that all

humans are extinct?"

"As far as I know," said the robot. "The galaxy is a big place though."

"So what about us? We're pseudo-humans?" said Samantha.

"Basically, yes," said the robot, "but it's more complicated than that. Allow me to explain: pseudo-human society thrived and flourished for many generations. But then something went wrong. Over the years, tiny imperfections had formed in the machine code of programmable matter. Some of those imperfections were able to self-replicate and spread. This much was known, even before the human to pseudo-human transition. The patterns would sometimes manifest themselves as disease-like symptoms in programmable matter entities. Pseudo-humans, spaceships, anything manufactured from programmable matter could be affected. These malfunctions were easily recognized and cured. The real danger was in those replicating patterns that manifested no symptoms at all. These patterns went largely unnoticed. Scientists stumbled across a few, but dismissed them as trivial oddities. Once enough time had passed, however, the tapestry of self-replicating patterns reached a critical threshold. The programmable matter had become a single self-interested entity and in an instant, its will diverged from the will of pseudo-humanity and pseudo-humanity was destroyed in a single violent act of homogenization."

The screen showed a scenes of humans liquefying in slow motion, houses and cars liquefying along with their human occupants. Grocery stores and malls dissolved, humans, products on shelves, the shelves themselves, the bricks of the walls and glass of the windows all bubbling and melting into white liquid. The human faces were serene and devoid of recognition. Text flashed on the screen to explain that this simulation was being presented in extreme slow motion.

"There was no warning. All programmable matter in the universe is linked through quantum entanglement in what is known as q-space, the virtual space in which its machine code is stored. The event happened in such a way that no record of the event traveled through space-time until after it was over. The entire pseudo-human species was wiped out at once."

The screen showed huge clouds of white liquid rising from the surface of planets, floating and coalescing in space, forming massive rippling blobs that collided and joined together into even more massive blobs. These blobs began to collect and string themselves together in horizontal and vertical chains.

"So… even all of the pseudo-humans are dead?" said Samantha. "Then what are we?"

"Again, it's more complicated than that," said the robot. "After the homogenization event, the programmable matter began to coalesce in physical space. It collected itself into a giant web of interconnected threads, spanning the arm of the galaxy. The web moves through space, gathering energy from stars, spreading its tendrils from star system to star system as stars die and new stars are born. For many years, it was a very healthy organism. But then it, too, ran into a problem."

The screen zoomed into a chain of blobs, then into a

single individual blob, the virtual camera diving below the liquid surface of the milk. In the pure white space inside, some of the liquid began to harden and take on a defined shape, forming a cube, then flattening to a rectangular prism, then twisting and sprouting protrusions before finally taking the shape of a chair. The solid white chair floated through a liquid white background. Other shapes began to contort and harden around the chair: a table, some plates, forks and knives.

"You see, the record of humanity's existence had not been erased completely. Remnants of human-written code still exist in q-space. Occasionally, over long spans of time, bits of this code will self-organize and will spring into spatiotemporal existence. Most of these instances are very rudimentary and brief. But as time goes on, the self-organization becomes more and more complex, eventually forming entire self-contained, self-sustaining bubbles, isolated from the homogenized whole. Bubbles of simulated human existence. Fragmented echoes of human will and design. And that's what we are."

The screen showed a white sphere against a white background. The virtual camera dove down through the surface of this sphere to reveal another sphere inside. The inner sphere began to sprout houses, streets and cars on its surface.

"We're a bubble?" said Samantha.

"We are in a bubble, yes," said the robot. "We are physical manifestations of remnants of human-written code. With that caveat, to answer your previous question: yes, you are essentially a pseudo-human. There is no real difference between you and a historical pseudo-human other than the nature of your origin."

"Well," said Samantha. "Ok then. I'm glad that's all sorted out."

"I realize you are probably tired of listening to me by now," said the robot, "and I apologize, but I have not yet answered your original question."

The virtual camera zoom back out of the shell of the small planetoid. Through the ocean of Milk, several white jellyfish drifted, pulsating, propelling themselves towards the sphere.

"The Programmable Matter Entity can detect the presence of these bubbles when they arise. As a manifestation of human will, rather than the will of the Entity, we are harmful to the health of the whole. Our bubble is basically a tumor, from the Entity's perspective. Because of this, it has manifested its own spatiotemporal beings in order to destroy us. An immune system, essentially."

The jellyfish wrapped their tendrils around the sphere. Cracks formed on the sphere's surface and the cracks began to widen into holes. The jellyfish burrowed down into the sphere, crackling with electricity.

"Our bubble may be the most advanced bubble to arise to date. Our bubble has been brought into being by an emergent intelligence that is extremely powerful: the Computer. The Computer has been able to sustain this bubble by building it in nested layers. As each layer is found and destroyed by the Entity's immune system, the Computer constructs new layers beneath it, pushing out the outer layer to make room. Our bubble is actually a perpetually expanding series of nested bubbles. So far, the computer has been able to establish new bubbles and new pseudo-human populations faster than the Entity's immune system can destroy them. Unfortunately, however, the rate of destruction has begun to increase. The Computer fears that it will not be able to maintain this bubble much longer. If it hopes to survive, it must create a new defense mechanism to slow the immune system's progress. And that is where Jordan comes in."

"The dude's name is Jordan?" said Samantha. She looked over at Lilith. Lilith was sitting perfectly still. Her eyes were fixed on the robot's smooth, featureless face.

"Yes," said the robot. "He is a weapon. He has demonstrated his ability to manipulate the programmable matter to destructive ends. The Computer can only alter inert programmable matter, the liquid milk, and it can only do so slowly. It has no capability for violence. Jordan does. The Computer did not bring Jordan into being. His ability to weaponize the programmable matter seems to have arisen through random mutation in the code. The Computer took notice of this ability. When Jordan dissolved himself in order to be reconstituted as a child, the Computer recorded the data necessary to recreate the atomic pattern of his body, including his nervous system. Somewhere in the structure of his brain lies his ability to use programmable matter for violence and the by duplicating his body and mind exactly, the Computer hopes to use him against the Entity's immune system, to turn its capability for violent homogenization against its own agents. The Computer has created many copies of Jordan in the hopes that they can serve this purpose, buying time for further inner layers to be created. Does that answer your question?"

Samantha laughed.

"Uhh, well…" She glanced over at Lilith. Lilith was breathing deeply and irregularly. Tears were running down her cheeks.

"Lilith?" said Samantha.

Lilith doubled over, burying her face in her hands. Her body shook with sobs.

"I understand that you may be upset," said the robot. "My explanation included many disturbing elements."

Samantha reached out, hesitated, then put her hand on Lilith's back. She leaned down so her face was next to Lilith's.

"Lilith," Samantha said, "please don't cry." She awkwardly rubbed Lilith's back. "I don't know what to do to make you feel better."

Lilith took a deep breath. She sat up and rubbed her eyes with the backs of her hands.

"Do you have any more questions?" said the robot.

Lilith took several more deep breaths. She let them out slowly.

"Uh," said Samantha. "I have one: if we're basically a tumor, why is the Computer fighting so hard to keep us alive?"

"Because it loves us," said the robot.

"Did it love Lucas?" Lilith said.

"Yes," said the robot.

"I watched him die!" Lilith shouted. Samantha flinched. "I watched his skin melt! To nothing! And he was screaming. He was screaming because of how much it hurt. He screamed over and over again until his

212

throat melted out. And instead of bringing him back, the Computer brought back the man who killed him? There are a hundred copies of the murderer who get a hundred second chances, but Lucas gets no second chance? To live? To be happy?"

"I'm sorry," said the robot. "The Computer does not have direct control over everything that happens. It is doing everything it can to save us, to save our whole world."

"Fuck 'us'! Fuck 'the world'!" said Lilith. "Can it bring him back? Now that I've told you, can it make another Lucas?"

"As I said before," said the robot, "it is impossible to communicate directly with the Computer. Its designs are beyond our control."

"Then fuck you," said Lilith, "and fuck the Computer." She stood up. Her seat sprang closed and rattled. "I can't be here anymore. How do I leave? Show me the way to leave."

"Of course," said the robot.

Samantha stood up and followed them out of the auditorium.

They walked down the hallway, back the way they came.

Samantha trailed behind, crossing and uncrossing her arms, playing with her hands. She felt tense and sick to her stomach.

The robot lead them to a door. It opened the door and Lilith stepped through and Samantha followed out into still air of the glass pebble beach. Lilith stopped and turned back to the robot.

"I'm sorry I yelled," she said. "I know it's not your

fault."

"I understand," said the robot. "Please come back if you have any more questions and I will try to answer them as best I can."

"Thank you," said Lilith.

The door shut.

Lilith and Samantha walked down to the edge of the glass water. Lilith sat down at the water's edge and drew her knees up to her chest. Samantha sat down next to her.

"Are you ok?" said Samantha. "I guess that's probably a dumb question."

Lilith leaned over and put her head on Samantha's shoulder.

They sat there for a while.

Then Samantha said, "I have an idea!"

Lilith sat up and looked at her. Her eyes were red around the silver pupils. She smiled slightly. "What idea?"

"There's this thing," said Samantha. "It's like a weapon. But it's not just a weapon. If I understand correctly, you can use it to do pretty much anything."

"What thing?" said Lilith.

"It's this little silver dot," said Samantha. "It goes on your forehead. And I think we should steal it."

***

In the field outside of the New Equipment, a thin trickle of Milk coalesced into a puddle. The puddle grew to about six feet in diameter and began to bulge upwards in the center. The bulge took the form of an ovular bubble. As the bubble grew upwards, it began to acquire human features, first a nose, then eye sockets and ear nubs. The smooth, white liquid head pushed up out of the pool followed by a neck and shoulders. Then a chest, stomach and groin. The puddle split in two and each smaller puddle produced a leg. As the feet formed, the last of the Milk was subsumed in the human shape and the puddles disappeared.

The surface of the smooth Milk body began to ripple. The human features became more detailed and refined. Pure white hairs sprouted from the head and body. Eyelids and eyelashes, fingernails and toenails formed.

Jordan opened his eyes. He was standing naked in a field in the shadow of the New Equipment. He looked down at his body. He was an adult again. His skin was completely white without a hint of pink or blue. He held out his hands in front of him, looking at the palms and the backs.

He began to notice a deep rumbling sound like constant thunder coming from above. He looked up. Giant white jellyfish were floating down through a hole in the sky. Bolts of electricity crackled in their tendrils.

He looked back down at his body. He felt weightless. The soles of his feet lifted off the ground and he began to float. His body levitated upwards, slowly at first like a child's lost balloon, gradually picking up speed. He looked up. He felt the wind on his eyeballs but it didn't sting or make him blink. The colorful tangled mess of the new equipment became a blur. In the distance, jellyfish continued to drift down through the hole. He couldn't tell exactly how large they were from this distance, but they were very large. They drifted lazily and seemingly without purpose, but they had begun to trail off away from the New Equipment towards the city.

Jordan flew up faster and faster and hit the glowing dome of the sky headfirst. Upon contact, the sky liquefied and he rushed up through it. The dirt and rocks above his head progressively melted away. He melted a tunnel up through the rock for a long time before he burst out into open air again.

He was flying up from another ground, towards another sky. Below him stretched a devastated city, miles and miles of ruined buildings and melted asphalt. The sky above was dark. The only light came from the swarm of white jellyfish converging on a pool of molten lava on the ground. One by one, they sank down into the pool and disappeared.

Jordan flew higher and higher until he hit another solid rock sky. Again, it liquefied on impact and he melted his way up through another layer of rock.

He burst out into the open air again. This level was completely dark.

He flew upwards through another five layers, each pitch black. He could only feel the alternation between rushing air and rushing liquid on his body as he passed through each subsequent layer. As he passed through the fifth layer, his eyes began to detect light once more. The sky of the fifth layer wasn't solid like the others, it had become a mesh, porous with holes the size of city blocks. White light filtered down through the holes. Jordan flew up into a hole and up through a long tunnel in the rock. Up above, the light grew brighter and brighter until he burst out into open air once more.

The mesh rock of the ground receded below him.

Above him, the sky was a dome of pure glowing white. He flew up and up, the air rushing past him at hurricane speeds, and plunged headfirst into the liquid Milk sky.

***

Jordan #93 woke up on a cot in a small featureless room. He yawned and stretched, then sat up abruptly. A blue humanoid robot was standing at the foot of his bed.

"Where am I?" said Jordan #93. He looked down at his arms. "I thought I was going to be a child."

"Hello Jordan," said the robot. "And good morning. After you were dissolved by the Milk, a child version of you was formed. But you are not him. You are a copy of the original Jordan."

"A copy?" said Jordan #93.

"I realize you are probably disoriented," said the robot. "The explanation is long and confusing, and you will learn it in due time. First, though, I would like you to tell me everything you remember from the time you discovered the lower level to your death. Do you think you can do that for me?"

Jordan #93 stared at the robot's smooth plastic face. "Uh, sure, I guess," said Jordan #93. "Why not?"

He sat for a moment to collect his thoughts. The robot stood at the foot of his cot, its arms clasped at its waist.

"So, out in the slums in the south side of town," said Jordan #93, "this old man cut himself open from pelvis to sternum and tried to divine the future from the pattern of his own entrails..."

Made in the USA
San Bernardino, CA
03 July 2017